Bandits, Bears, and Backaches

Bandits, Bears, and Backaches:
A Collection of Short Stories
Based on Arkansas History

By

Velma B. Branscum Woody

Butler Center for Arkansas Studies
Central Arkansas Library System
2004

Woody, Velma B. Branscum.
    Bandits, bears, and backaches : a collection of short stories based on
Arkansas history / by Velma B. Branscum Woody.
    xiv, 79 p. ; 23 cm.

Copyright © 2004 by Butler Center for Arkansas Studies

Library of Congress Catalog Card Number: 2004111848
ISBN 978-0-9708574-2-2

First published in 2004
First Edition

Butler Center for Arkansas Studies, Central Arkansas Library System, 100 Rock Street, Little Rock, AR 72201

Printed in the United States of America

The paper used in this book complies with the Permanent Paper Standard issued by the National Information Standards Organization (Z39.48-1984).

Cover illustration: From *Wild Sports in the Far West* by Frederick Gerstaecker, 1859.

Bandits, Bears, and Backaches: A Collection of Short Stories Based on Arkansas History

Contents

Foreword ....*page xi*

I.   The Mastodon Kill.. *page 1*

II.   Bears and Panthers Aplenty: Early Settlers
         Make a Home Arkansas...*page 7*

III.   The Museum of Gray Sky...*page 15*

IV.   Mary and the Red River Raft.....................................*page 21*

V.   Arkansas Civil War Bandits and Outlaws.....................*page 29*

VI.   Bass Reeves: Great Lawman of the West.....................*page 37*

VII.   The 1927 Flood..*page 43*

VIII. Sunburns and Sore Muscles: Working to Save the
         Farm During the Great Depression.........................*page 49*

IX.   Timber: Living and Working in an
         Arkansas Forest..*page 57*

X.   Japanese Americans and the Rohwer
         Relocation Camp..*page 63*

XI.   To the North: A Black Family Leaves Arkansas
         to Find Work in Michigan.......................................*page 71*

This volume is dedicated to
Mamie Trammell Branscum
(1925-1986)

Acknowledgements

I wish to thank my family, who worked so diligently to help me create this book, and Tom W. Dillard, Curator of the Butler Center, who was so patient and helpful throughout this process.

I especially want to thank my parents, Thurlow and Mamie Branscum, as well as Charlie Branscum, my Grandfather, who gave me the love of history, especially Arkansas history.

Foreword

Arkansas history is fascinating. Our state has a long and complex history, one that is full of interesting people, exciting events, amazing accomplishments, and a great deal of heartbreak. The purpose of this book is to provide students with a collection of stories that will put a human face on the history of our state and its people.

Our history is about people. These stories tell how Arkansans—from the earliest Indians on down to the modern era—have built lives here in what is today known as Arkansas.

All too often Arkansas history is told in terms of politics, business, and wars. This book will help students realize that behind all these larger events are the lives of average people. These stories are like "windows into the past," which I hope will enable students to better understand our history and the generations of Arkansans who have worked to build our state.

It is important to realize that these stories are fictional, but based on known historical fact. I hope the stories will encourage students to study Arkansas history with a little more enthusiasm—and with a realization that they too are a part of the story of our state.

Tom W. Dillard
Curator
Butler Center for Arkansas Studies
Central Arkansas Library System

The Mastodon Kill

Wyum was walking ahead of the small band of Paleo-Indians as they traveled through the dense forest surrounding a huge river. Even in the daylight hours, a heavy blanket of fog enveloped the entire area. The fog was a sign that the cold months were fast approaching. The band was looking for a cave or large overhanging bluff to provide shelter for the long cold months of winter that lay just ahead. Wyum was twelve winters old. He had just had his rites of manhood ceremony and he planned to hunt with his band this year.

Wyum was walking fast as he cleared the woods and strode into the sandy gravel of the riverbed. He followed the river for a while, daydreaming as he walked. Suddenly, he realized that he was alone at the foot of a large ravine near the river. Enormous currents due to severe flooding down through the ages had cut this large ditch in the river silt. As Wyum neared the ravine he noticed that driftwood and fallen timber lined the giant ditch.

The ravine was dark and gloomy especially surrounded with so much fog. The air felt heavy with unknown spirits. Ancient trees with bulging roots looked like live beings in the heavy fog. Huge piles of driftwood surrounded the ditch and exposed boulders were visible in the giant hole. Small bushes and broken tree limbs protruded in all directions. Misty fog swirled above the water. The sounds of the river seemed to be everywhere, echoing off cliffs and seeming to move the shadows of the early morning.

Wyum walked closer as he noticed some of the driftwood begin to move. His heart was racing as he silently crept closer and closer. He wondered what he would find in the scary pit.

He was amazed to see a huge mastodon bull lying on its side, trapped in the ravine. The large animal was almost covered by the debris, and it was clearly trying to get to its feet. The huge mastodon had fallen into the gorge and had broken his left front leg. Wyum could see the protruding bone as the trapped animal tried to move about looking for a way to escape. But, he could not get out! His leg would not support his weight. Wyum turned and ran back to get his band.

While Wyum was out exploring, his band had stopped under a huge overhanging limestone bluff jutting out over the face of a cliff. They had decided to camp there to explore for more permanent lodging before the long cold began. They were very tired and needed a few days rest. They had hoped to find game and wild birds to supplement their diet to give them strength to face the winter months.

Bog, the band's leader, began to explore. When he entered the overhang he realized that a cave was hidden in the giant rock. The cave opening was narrow, but inside he found one fairly large cave room. It would be sufficient for a band that now consisted of fourteen people including three small babies. Preserving the band was all that mattered. They had lost five members this year due to accidents and sickness.

Bog looked for signs of wild animals such as bear or panther or other dangerous beasts. All he found were a few old bones, probably left over from kill made by a bear or panther. This would be a wonderful shelter for his people. They could fish, and kill water birds and even bigger animals that came to the river to drink. Bog ran to tell the band they had found shelter.

Just as Bog ran to get his band members, Wyum came running down the riverbed to tell of his exciting find. Wyum was jumping and waving his hands, pointing upstream, too eager to communicate properly. Finally, Wyum calmed down enough to explain what he had found.

Bog and the other four men followed Wyum to the gorge. They were talking and gesturing, planning excitedly as they walked. The women stayed behind to clean the cave and set up the hearth. Excited by finding the cave, they were anxious to make a home for the band.

Wyum took the men straight to the trapped mastodon. For a long time they watched the beast, trying to determine how best to slaughter it. They were laughing and gesturing, more excited than they had been in months.

Upon returning, the men found that the women had cleaned the cave and lined the floor with sweet smelling grasses and leaves. They had carried flat rocks into the cave to make a hearth for warmth and cooking. They were cooking a few large rabbits over a blazing fire.

The men ate at the hearth, excitedly telling the women and children of their wonderful find. After eating, they sat around the hearth planning how to go about slaughtering the trapped mastodon. This would prove dangerous if they did not develop the right strategy.

Because there were only five men, this task was huge. They would have to kill the beast with their spears and then bring as much meat to the shelter as possible. This small band could never preserve and keep the whole animal. What the band could not carry, other scavengers would devour. Wolves and other wild animals would appear quickly. Even buzzards would make an appearance soon after the kill. They would have to devise a plan to bring their meat back to the shelter before the other animals arrived on the scene. Otherwise, they might have to fight off the hungry wolves, especially after sunset.

The men prepared their sharpest spears for the kill. The women and children would also go to help with the butchering and carry the meat. Luckily, the cave wasn't very far away. They might even make two trips.

That would be all the meat they could use before it would spoil. But, they would have fresh meat for many days. The sharp spear points and knives would speed up the butchering process. They also took their stone axes to break bones to get at the nutritious marrow inside.

The next morning the band left the shelter at daybreak. They arrived at the gorge in just a short time. The men went to the edge of the ravine and peered down. The injured and trapped animal continued his pathetic attempts to find a way out of the gorge. Wyum, being the youngest male, and his cousin, Wok, who was two years older, were chosen to guard the mouth of the gorge to be certain the animal could not escape.

The men walked slowly and carefully as they positioned themselves on all sides of the bellowing beast. They each had a spear raised, ready to attack.

Bog began the slaughter by throwing his spear, aiming at the eye of the trapped beast. This spear went astray and glanced off the mastodon's gigantic tusks.

The other three men also threw their spears. One spear went into the throat, while another went under the shoulder blade, landing near the heart. The last spear lodged in the ribcage. The mighty pachyderm gave a terrible roar as it sank down.

The hunters smiled broadly as they cautiously moved toward the dying beast. As quickly as a bolt of lightening and with his last reserve of energy, the mastodon rose again and lunged at its attackers. Bog, who was at the front of the approaching band, was caught by the beast's tusks as it fell once again upon the ground. The animal was in its death throes, but Bog was trapped under the huge ivory tusks.

Bog was screaming from fear and the weight of the huge tusk that was slowly but surely crushing his leg. Wyum and Wok reacted immediately, jumping into the ravine and hacking at the heavy tusks with their stone axes. Soon the boys had Bog freed. They and the other band members helped him to the river where they bathed his badly swollen leg.

While Bog's injuries were serious, his leg was not broken. Wyum helped Bog return to camp, while the rest of the band began butchering the giant animal.

After quickly opening the carcass with their sharp stone knives, the men removed the heart. Each hunter ate a portion of the heart as a way of honoring the animal that had just forfeited its life. This would provide magical strength for those who honored the animal. They then began to cut the meat into large pieces, which they hurriedly gave to the women and children to carry back to the cave. Working quickly, the men used their sharp stone tools to cut off as much meat as possible. They could hear the wolves growling as they impatiently awaited their turn at the carcass.

Finally, as the sun set behind the mountain, the weary hunters started for their shelter, their backs laden with the last load of the warm red meat.

That night as they sat around the cooking fire, the hunters recounted the adventures of the day. This bounty of meat would last them a long time.

Maybe, then the spirits would send deer or elk to help them survive the cold months ahead. They had found a very good place to stay. Their small band could survive. As long as there was a band, there was life. As long as there was life, there was hope.

Suggested Reading:

Frank Shambach and Leslie Newell, *Crossroads of the Past: 12,000 Years of Indian Life in Arkansas*. North Little Rock: Arkansas Endowment for the Humanities, 1990.

George Sabo, III, "Native American Prehistory," in Jeannie M. Whayne, *et al., Arkansas: A Narrative History*. Fayetteville: University of Arkansas Press, 2002, pp. 1-19.

Bears and Panthers Aplenty: Early Settlers Make a Home in Arkansas

Nick pushed his spurs into the sides of the huge mare as she hurried up the lane to his Tennessee home. He could hardly wait to see his family. He had been away from home for three months. Nick had helped blaze the Southwest Trail down through the new state of Arkansas. He loved the area, especially around the new settlement of Arkadelphia. Arkansas had been a state for four years. Nick decided in the early spring of 1840 to make a trip to Arkadelphia to homestead land. Ever since his trailblazing days, he had wanted a place at the end of the Southwest Trail. His dream was finally coming true.

David, now twelve years old and his fourteen-year old brother Daniel were hoeing in the garden, with Ma's help. Raymond, who was the older brother, now eighteen years of age, was in the woods cutting timber. David and Daniel heard the pounding of the mare's hooves coming up the lane. They looked at each other.

"Pa's home," they yelled at the same time. "Pa's home."

The boys dropped their hoes and ran to the house. Ma was close behind.

Nick threw the mare's reins over the fence and jumped to the ground. He grabbed the boys in a powerful hug and then he looked up and saw Ma.

"Nick," whispered Ma. "I am so glad you are home."

"I'm glad to be home too, Anna," Nick sighed.

The boys were clamoring for attention. They were both talking at once.

"Calm down boys. We will have plenty of time to talk later. Right now all I want is some good food to eat and rest my sore bones," Pa said.

Just then Maggie their three-year-old daughter awoke from her nap.

"Papa, Papa!" cried Maggie, "Hold me, Hold me."

Pa grabbed Maggie, laughing and swinging her in the air.

Ma prepared a wonderful supper and the entire family celebrated. After the meal, Pa began to talk.

"Anna, you and the children know how hard the last few years have been. We have lost much of the livestock to disease. Some years hailstorms have destroyed the crops, while every year it seems that farms prices fall lower and lower. I have put on a brave face, but most of the time life has been very hard for all of us. While I was out, I claimed a homestead of 640 acres in Arkansas near the new settlement of Arkadelphia. This town is located in southwest Arkansas. This territory is very beautiful. I know you all will love it there."

"Nick," asked Ma, "how are we going to prepare for the trip? Where will the money come from?"

"Well," replied Pa, "I thought we would sell everything here and buy a couple of wagons and supplies. We can preserve all the fruits and veg-etables for the next month or so. I'll hunt and we can salt down the meat. It will be a lot of work but I think we can manage if we are real careful."

Ma was silent for a few minutes. She then lifted her head and looked at the children.

"Looks like we have work to do," said Ma simply.

The family worked hard for the next couple of months. They sold the farm and most of their posses-sions.

They began their journey from

From: *Big Bear of Arkansas* by Thomas Bangs Thorpe, 1858

Wayne County, Tennessee on July 14, 1840. They traveled over mostly flat land. The trip was long and tiring. Pa broke the monotony by telling tales around the campfire each night. One night, after a particularly exhausting day, they ate a supper of dried venison and vegetables. The meal was good, but they all wanted fresh meat. Pa and the boys didn't want to hunt until they crossed the river on the ferry into Arkansas because the wilderness offered better game. Pa leaned back to rest when he heard a squeak from the bushes.

"What was that Pa?" asked Maggie, fear sounding in her voice.

"I think it was a snake killing a field mouse." Pa said.

"Pa," whispered Maggie, "I'm afraid of snakes!"

"Well, you should be afraid of them honey," Pa said sharply, "and you must be very careful and watch closely for them."

Pa moved around to a more comfortable position; cradling Maggie in his arms he began to speak.

"One day about a year ago, I was helping to blaze a trail going from south Arkansas over into Louisiana. The area was swampy and snakes and lizards were all around.

"Now, I have always respected snakes and been somewhat leery of them. I watched out for them as I cleared brush and cut trees. About noon, I decided to stop and eat a little snack. I stopped near a beautiful spring. The wild grasses surrounded the water and the bright sunlight made it look like paradise on earth. I ate my food slowly, savoring every bite. I rested for a few minutes then decided to drink from the sparkling spring. I lay down on the wild grasses and drank deeply from the bubbling water. I stood up to leave and then heard something on the ground. To my horrified amazement, I saw that I had been lying on a rattlesnake. I will never know why that snake didn't bite me. I just turned and left. I didn't have the heart to kill the snake. After all it had chosen to let me live. I don't know if I made the right decision or not but I'll never forget that rattler."

The children sat quietly. They could think of nothing to say. Ma told them it was time for bed and they didn't resist. Ma and Pa smiled as they watched each child carefully search their bedroll before they lay down.

The next day went quietly and that evening they arrived at the ferry. They would board the ferry early the next morning. They could hardly wait.

They crossed the river by ferry on July 31, 1840. David and Daniel stood silently, staring at the churning waters surrounding the ferryboat that was slowly inching across the huge Mississippi River. David looked back at their two wagons being carried on the ferry. His mother sat on one wagon, his father on the other. Upon reaching the riverbank, the wagons were quickly driven onto dry ground.

Soon they found the perfect camping spot near a little creek running from a spring just over the hill from the ferry landing. Ma set her spider kettle over the fire Pa made as soon as they arrived. She cut up some venison jerky and put it into water taken from the spring.

She then added some of the dried vegetables and a few potatoes, adding a touch of salt pork for flavor. She sat and stirred the stew, while Pa napped. They all enjoyed a good supper.

As they sat by the campfire, they heard the lonely howling of a wolf pack. Pa sat quietly for a moment then began to speak about how he came to have his dog.

"I was blazing a road near the Texas border three years ago last summer. One evening as I was returning to camp, I heard something whimpering in the bushes. I knew it wasn't a dangerous animal so I investigated the sound. I looked under some thick vines and found one solitary little wolf puppy. Evidently the mama had died from starvation because I could see the body nearby."

Pa continued, "The little wolf puppy looked so sad. He didn't seem dangerous. I knew he was going to die. I turned to leave when I heard him cry out again. I turned back and the little fellow was trying to follow me. I dug into my saddlebag and gave him a little piece of meat. He ate the food from my hand then licked my fingers. I decided to take him with me. I put him inside my coat. I fed him morsels of what I ate. He began to grow. I decided to name him Whimper. He still follows me everywhere I go. Still, when I hear a wolf howl, I am afraid he will leave."

David and Daniel looked at each other, then at Whimper. He seemed to be resting peacefully unaware that his cousins were calling to him. Every once in a while he would open one eye and look around at the family, then go back to sleep.

David said, "I don't think Whimper wants to leave."

Daniel replied, "I don't either. He seems perfectly content. I sure hope the wolf pack can't lure him away."

Just then a lone wolf howled. Whimper perked up his ears, then ran and hid in Daniel's bedroll. The boys heard a small whimper as the wolf burrowed his head in the bedding. Laughing loudly, David said he was convinced Whimper was there to stay.

The following morning everyone arose early, ate breakfast, and started the next part of their journey. They were more rested and couldn't wait to be on their way.

As the two wagons lumbered on, the terrain began to change. They saw thick heavy timber and hills that were rocky and steep in many places. Pa had to scout out the trail every day to make sure they could pass through the deep dark hollows and an occasional creek.

The wagons rocked dangerously on some of the terrain and it required every muscle and bone in the entire family to keep the young horses on the trail. The family had been on the trail since the middle of July. It was now the first of September. They were hot and tired, and the dried food was no longer appetizing.

They were all hungry for fresh food. Pa decided to stop for a few days and hunt for some fresh game. Pa knew they could not take the time to preserve the meat, but he felt they all deserved some fresh food. He also hoped the fresh grass and rest would help the horses make the last leg of the journey.

Two days later, Pa pulled the lead wagon over to a little creek in a wooded area. A beautiful meadow lined one side of the creek and a canebrake lined the other. Pa was always leery of canebrakes so he cautioned everybody to be extra careful. He knew that these large fields of native bamboo often hid huge bears and panthers that were very dangerous.

David and his brothers and sister were happy to rest. Ma, with Maggie by her side, began to unpack food from the wagons for supper tonight. The food rations, especially the meat, were running low. Weevils had infested some of the flour and cornmeal.

Everybody was tired and a little depressed. Ma had even stopped singing along the trail. Maggie was cranky and had itchy bumps from the ticks and mosquitoes. The grownups had fared no better. While the grownups napped, David, Daniel, and Raymond grabbed some twine and ran up the creek as fast as possible to catch some fish.

Fishing always relaxed the boys. David and his brothers cooled off in the creek and then began to fish. They each cut a cane pole, tied a string to the pole, and used worms to bait their hooks. Soon the fish began to bite. In about an hour, the boys had enough fish for supper and even for lunch the next day. They strung their fish on a small limb cut from a willow tree near the creek. David was carrying the fish back to camp.

Just as they rounded a bend near the campsite, they heard a scream. It sounded exactly like a woman screaming in agony. The brothers knew they were hearing the cry of a hungry panther. The scream sounded very close. David caught a glimpse of something moving in the canebrake across the creek.

Their hearts pounding with fear, the boys ran toward camp. David thought the hungry beast smelled the fresh fish. They could see the cane shake and they feared the panther was following closely. They sighed with relief when they reached camp and found Pa rubbing down the horses.

They quietly walked into the camp. David smiled broadly at his brothers. He felt like a pioneer at last. They would never tell of the scare they had in the canebrake. Instead, they sank down in the grass, exhausted, and fell asleep waiting for the fish to cook.

After a wonderful supper of fried fish, the family sang for a while near the campfire, and then went to bed. Pa took the first watch. He would guard the camp until one o'clock, then Raymond would take the watch for the remainder of the night. The family rested the next day. They swam, fished some more, napped and slowly regained their strength after their already perilous and tiring journey.

The third day, Pa and the boys scouted the woods for deer. They knew the deer would come to the creek around dusk or in the early morning dawn to drink. They had studied the creek bank for deer tracks for a couple of days and knew where they went to get water. Today was the day to hunt. Pa and the boys started just before dawn. Walking slowly and quietly, the hunters made their way to the creek.

They saw a herd of eight deer drinking from the pool. Fortunately, they were "down wind" of the deer—so the animals could not smell them. The deer were drinking and frolicking in the water. Daniel drew a bead on one of the huge bucks on the outside of the group. Raymond aimed for a barely grown buck just a few steps behind.

Both deer went down at the same time. The huge boom from the guns sounded like only one shot. Pa and the boys returned to camp with their bounty of meat. They had killed two deer that day, and they feasted for a week on the kill.

A week later, the family was on the trail again. The next three weeks were uneventful, except for their daily encounters with snakes and mosquitoes. Pa thought they were about three days away from their homestead. They camped near a beautiful spring. The nights were much cooler now and

Pa wanted to get to the homestead as soon as possible, so he and the boys could build a cabin before the arrival of winter.

Pa was restless, feeling the need to press on. He took the first watch as always. David had curled up next to the wagon so he could listen to his mother and sister sing. Ma sang softly so that all would sleep better that night. Suddenly, Pa yelled. He didn't exactly scream, but it was warning enough.

Raymond jumped up with his gun ready, grabbed the lantern hanging by the campfire, and ran toward the noise. They were shocked and amazed at the sight before them when Raymond held the lantern high. A huge black bear had Pa in a grip that looked exactly like he was hugging him. Pa's rifle had fallen to the ground and the bear was hopping around on two feet like he was dancing a waltz.

Pa was pounding on the bear's chest, screaming for help.

At that moment, Raymond jumped at the bear's back. His knife was in his hand, and he stabbed the beast with all his strength. He stabbed the monster in the back, sides and under the shoulder. Still the bear held on, biting at Pa's shoulders all the while. Daniel jumped in and with a lucky strike, hit a vein in the bear's throat.

The animal held on to Pa for a few slow seconds, then slowly loosened his grip and sank to the ground. Raymond and Daniel grabbed Pa and helped him up. Pa was weak from the loss of blood, and the boys were afraid that his ribs were broken. But, at least he was still breathing. The boys took him back to the camp, where Ma cleaned and bandaged his wounds. For over a week Pa lay on his bedroll as Ma tended his wounds. Finally, Pa arose and insisted that he was fine and wanted to move on although he walked stiffly and painfully. They travelled slowly for a few days, giving Pa time to heal.

The remainder of the trip took two weeks instead of the three days that Pa had predicted. Finally, they arrived in Arkadelphia. Pa had recovered and he and the boys worked fast to build a new home.

Winter was near and a cabin had to be built. The family chose a beautiful spot surrounded by tall pine trees. A bubbling spring spilled into a brook just behind the cabin site. Ma wouldn't have to worry about a water supply. The place was perfect. Pa and Raymond cut the trees with axes and saws. They were very careful to cut each log the right length and width so the cabin would be warm.

David and Daniel gathered flat rocks for the foundation and fireplace. Together the family raised the cabin in less than two weeks. The roof was made of wide shingles cut from a straight oak tree. The cabin had one large living room, which included a fireplace for cooking, a large sleeping room, and two sleeping spaces in the loft. Their home was warm and snug. They were ready for winter. The settlers from Tennessee had a home on the Arkansas frontier at last.

Suggested Reading:

Nancy Maxwell, "Born to Lead: Jacob Pyeatt and the Journey to Arkansas," *Pulaski County Historical Review*, XXXVI (Winter 1988), pp. 74-81.

Skipper Steely, *Six Months from Tennessee…A Story of the Many Pioneers of Miller County, Arkansas….* Wolfe City, TX: Henington Pub. Co., 1982.

The Museum of Gray Sky

Dixie White Dove ran down the hallways of the Middle School buildings at Sequoyah High School in Tahlequah, Oklahoma. She was thirteen years old and in the eighth grade. The year was 2002. Dixie was excited because this was Friday. Next week Dixie's entire class was going to visit her grandmother, Gray Sky, at her Indian Museum near the Cherokee reservation. Most of the class members were Cherokees. The teacher, Mrs. Brown, planned for the class to spend the entire week researching and studying their heritage under the knowledgeable eyes of Gray Sky. They were to present an oral research report on their chosen piece of Cherokee history when they returned.

Gray Sky had started the little museum with the artifacts left from her long line of Cherokee ancestors. She had items from as far back as the Dwight Mission School near Russellville, Arkansas to the Civil War artifacts left from the First Cherokee Mounted Rifles, under the famous Confederate General Stand Watie.

Dixie had heard the stories of her ancestors at her Grandmother's museum all of her life. This time she wanted to share these stories with her friends and her classmates. Mrs. Brown thought this team research project would prove educational for the entire class.

Dixie ran to her friend, Amy, who was waiting for her on the school steps. Together, they walked to the car where Dixie's mother waited to drive them to the library to begin their research. Tomorrow, Dixie's mother would take the entire class by bus to Gray Sky's sprawling farm.

Early the next morning right after breakfast, the class started their tour of the museum. First, they viewed the artifacts brought from North

Carolina. Very few of these remained. Gray Sky showed them a headdress that belonged to an ancient shaman, who was Dixie's ancestor. She also had two large ceremonial pipes made from stone.

Next, Gray Sky went to the Dwight Mission display. She told them the story of her ancestor, Jonathan Hawk, who had been a student at Dwight Mission in 1822. She had an old, yellowed piece of paper—a letter written by Jonathan Hawk. She handed the paper to Dixie who read it aloud to her class. The top of the first page had been torn. The letter began:

August 18, 1842

My Dearest Love,

My father, John Hawk, thought I needed an education. We decided for me to go to Dwight Mission, a Christian School for Indians, near our home. We arrived at Dwight Mission on a cloudy day. We stood outside the fenced area of the school. The fence was huge. It probably enclosed twenty acres. These were four log structures and a schoolhouse. The schoolhouse was larger than the dwelling cabins.

I also saw two yokes of oxen, some cows and calves, hogs, and some farming equipment. My father and I were carefully studying the scene when, suddenly, out of one of the log houses came a very distinguished looking man. He was of average height with erect and graceful movements. He had the look of a man who was content with his place in life.

He strode directly to us with his hand out in a welcoming gesture. He was cheerful and seemed to want me to join his school. His voice was firm and his speech was honest and bold. He left no doubt of the sincerity and strength of his convictions. My father and I liked him at once. He introduced himself as Reverend Cephas Washburn, the founder of and missionary at Dwight Mission.

Mr. Washburn took me right into the building where the classes were held. He showed me the schedule that I was expected to keep. I was to go to school in the mornings and work on the mission farm in the afternoons.

I learned my schedule quickly enough and the farm work was not bad. But, I missed my parents and my old way of life. I could only see my parents on weekends. They did not like this either.

I liked reading, spelling, penmanship and geography. But, some of my instructors confused me with areas that I could not understand such as poetry. The main focus was on the gospel as well as the taming of "barbarians."

The adjustment was difficult. My friends and I hated our new surroundings. We were not used to the food. I stayed there two months. I learned some things that I hope will help me to have a better life. Still, I was happy to go home. I wanted to tell you of my past in a letter so you would understand why I am the man I am today. I hope this will explain the things that you have failed to understand. I hope to see you soon.

Love,
Jonathan Hawk

Dixie finished reading. The address of the person to whom the letter was sent was missing. Gray Sky just smiled. She knew the letter had been written to Jane White Doe who later became the wife of Jonathan Hawk. She explained this to the class. Gray Sky still had two of Jonathan's old school books.

One was a book of mathematics and one was the *Odyssey* by the Greek writer, Homer. The old books intrigued Dixie. She had tried to read them in the past and found her ancestor's study notes very interesting. She had always loved to learn about her ancestors.

Next, Gray Sky went to the Civil War artifacts. Here, she produced a Confederate uniform, a rifle and a sword.

"This uniform, rifle and sword belonged to Johnny Hawk who was Jonathan Hawk's son. He fought in the Civil War under the famous general, Stand Watie." Gray Sky explained.

Gray Sky leaned over a shelf and pulled a small black book from behind some other books.

"This is Johnny Hawk's diary. I do not

Sketch of Dwight Mission, 1824

display it to the public. But, since Dixie is his descendent, I would like her to read about the Civil War in Johnny's own words." Gray Sky sighed, handing the book to Dixie.

> April 20, 1863
> I have been in the Cherokee forces under General Stand Watie since August 9, 1861. Stand Watie organized a Cherokee regiment to fight for the Confederate cause. I am one of the original 300 solders to join the 1st Regiment, Cherokee Mounted Rifles. We have fought many fierce and bloody battles.
>
> We have continued to follow Stand Watie in battle after battle against the Union Armies. The food is scarce. We are eating mostly hard tack and jerky. I am hungry much of the time. We fight any way we can. We use our rifles, swords and often axes as clubs. We jump from trees onto our enemies. We fought to win any way we could ...I don't know if we did right, but it was the only way we knew....

Dixie stopped reading and reached for the glass of water Gray Sky held out to her. She drank deeply, and then scanned the diary for more passages. Many pages were blank or had been torn out. Dixie was saddened at the condition of the diary

"Grandmother, what happened to most of the pages," asked Dixie.

"Well, honey, unfortunately, through the many years, some of the pages fell out. Others were torn out before Johnny died. I guess someone didn't want some of the pages to be read. I've heard that some of it dealt with horrible executions," Gray Sky said sadly.

Dixie found another entry near the end of the book.

> April 27,1864
> "In this dreary spring of 1864, I have seen the Confederate Indian forces undergo a change in unit and command structure. The troops of the Creek and Seminole Nation's were brigaded with our Cherokee troops."
>
> "We just finished several fierce fights in Arkansas in the Red River Campaign. It seems only a matter of time until we must fight again. We will stand against the Federal Army

with nothing but our rifles and axes. When the battle is finished many of us will be gone. Now, we are supposed to be joined with the 1st and 2nd Creek Regiments. We are supposed to watch for supply boats heading up the Arkansas River from Fort Smith to Federal forces at Fort Gibson. Maybe there will be less fighting here. I don't think many of us can go on the way we are. We are sick and tired and soul weary. General Watie seems determined to stick with the Confederate cause."

"General Watie has good sense and is very cunning. He will employ all tactics available to win every battle. I think this is all that is keeping us going. I'll be glad when this awful war ends."

Dixie sighed as she lay the diary down. She looked at her grandmother. "You know Grandmother," I never realized that those soldiers had such a rough time," she commented with a frown on her face.

Gray Sky responded equally sadly, "Yes, it was a terrible time for everybody in the Civil War, regardless of which side one supported. That is the reason that I keep this little museum open. I hope to educate as many people as I can about our heritage, both Indian and American."

The eighth grade class left the museum intent on doing much more research through the week. They were looking forward to presenting an impressive report. The teacher was going to be pleasantly surprised.

Suggested Reading:

Edward E. Dale, "Arkansas and the Cherokees," *Arkansas Historical Quarterly*, VIII (Summer 1949), pp. 95-114.

Dorsey Jones, "Cephas Washburn and His Work in Arkansas," *Arkansas Historical Quarterly*, III (Summer 1944), pp. 125-136.

George Sabo, III, *Paths of Our Children: Historic Indians of Arkansas*. Fayetteville: Arkansas Archeological Survey, 1992.

Mary and The Red River Raft

Papa was excited last evening. He had read an interesting article in the *Red River Post*. The Arkansas Territorial Legislature had asked the U.S. Government to assign Henry Shreve with his snag boats to clear the Red River and make it useful for large boats. The settlers were all talking about the project. Mary was excited. She was thirteen years old and had lived on the river in the settlement of Fulton, Arkansas Territory, all her life. She could not wait to see the huge boats. She had heard of them from her Papa since she was little.

The "Red River Raft" was a thick mass of trees, brush, and debris, which fully covered one third of the surface of the Red River for 100 miles. For hundreds of years floods had slowly added to the raft, so that in some places the river was entirely blocked. In many places, this debris was so thick that it extended in a solid mass to the bottom of the river, often twenty-five feet deep. The debris made steamboat passage impossible.

A few weeks later, in February 1833, Papa read an article from a leading Little Rock paper confessing an oversight:

"We were not aware until within the last week that the United States snag boats under the charge of Captain Henry M. Shreve had been at work for the past three of four weeks in removing snags, sawyers, and other obstructions of the Arkansas River near Little Rock.

They are said to be making rapid progress in clearing the river of this impediment. Already they have removed most of the principal snags from the mouth of the river to the Pine Bluffs, a distance of more than 140 miles."

Papa laid the newspaper aside. "Papa" Mary begged. "Tell me about Henry Shreve. Who was he and how did he begin building boats?"

"Well, Mary, I have read some about Mr. Shreve. I believe he is a Quaker. He was reared on a farm in Pennsylvania near the Monongahela River. As a youngster he propelled a keelboat loaded with merchandise to St. Louis—a matter of 1,000 miles down the Ohio and 200 miles on the Mississippi—and returned with a load of furs, which he sold in Pittsburgh. He has always worked on the river and always navigated boats. He has great experience as a river pilot and navigator. He is the man for our job."

Mary sighed, "I wish I could meet Mr. Shreve. He seems so nice and knowledgeable."

"Yes," Papa agreed, "he is a great man I've been told."

This river clean up was Papa's dream. He wanted to see the mighty river cleared of all the debris that had held the channel captive for years upon years. That night at supper, Papa spoke excitingly about the arrival of the big boats. He said it would open up the area for steamboat traffic and should benefit everyone in southwest Arkansas Territory. Papa and many other people in the small town of Fulton could hardly wait for the snag boats to clear their part of the river.

"Papa," said an excited Mary, "I can't wait for them to get here. I want to go to the river to see them work."

"Oh, no! Mary!" Her father said, giving her a stern look. "You are to stay away from the river when they arrive. They will be using very dangerous equipment and dynamite. It is too dangerous for anybody especially a young girl. They will be blasting the river obstruction with very strong explosives. Listen to me—stay here with your Mama!"

Mary sighed as a cool breeze blew through the trees in the early June evening. The boats had finally arrived but Papa still refused to allow Mary to go to the river. She had been listening to the snag boats work all day. Oh, how she wished she were a boy! Had she been a boy, Papa would take her with him to see the gigantic snag boats at work. She might even be hired as an errand boy and actually ride on one of the snag boats as they cleared the massive raft.

Mary was so angry with her father. He never let her have any fun. All he wanted her to do was sit around doing nothing. Her life was so boring! Papa never allows me to have any fun, she said to herself. Mary fumed as she thought of how unfair and mean her father was to her.

Suddenly, Mary sat up. "That's it! I'll run away! I'll dress up like a boy and go down to the river and get a job on a snag boat. Papa will never know. He won't recognize me in boy's clothes with my hair pulled up under my hat," she thought. " I'll get the clothes from my cousin, Sam. He will never tell." Smiling broadly, Mary ran into the house to formulate her plan.

The next morning, Mary asked her mother if she could stay a few days with Aunt Sally, her mother's sister. Aunt Sally lived in Washington, Arkansas, the nearby county seat of Hempstead County. Mama said she could go.

Mary rushed to Uncle Johnny's farm to see Sam. He was nowhere to be found. Mary started for home, but she noticed some of his pants and a shirt hanging on the clothesline. She grabbed the clothes and ran. Sam wouldn't mind. She would explain everything later. She went home to finish packing. Mama came into the room just as Mary put the last garments in the bag.

"Mary, I thought you would have wanted to stay here since the snag boats are here." Mama said.

"Well, Papa won't let me go around the river while they are working. I thought if I was in Washington with Aunt Sally at least I wouldn't have to hear them if I can't see them." Mary said.

"I guess you're right." Mama said in a loving tone. "But Mary, Papa is only looking out for your best interest. You know he doesn't want you to get hurt."

"Yes, Mama, I know, but it just doesn't seem right—because I was born a girl I have to miss out on all the fun. I wish I had been a boy!"

Mama laughed and hugged Mary assuring her that one day she would be glad she wasn't a boy. Papa took Mary to Washington the next day. The trip took almost all day. Papa spent the night at Aunt Sally's and left early the following morning. As soon as he left, Mary asked Aunt Sally if she could go to see her friend Marian, who lived out in the country on a farm.

Aunt Sally agreed, though she was a bit confused, as she had looked forward to spending time with her niece.

Mary left Aunt Sally's and headed out of town. At the edge of town she sneaked into a barn and changed clothes. She dressed in Sam's pants and shirt. She pulled her long hair up and pinned it inside an old hat she had found on the street.

She caught her reflection in a store window. Mary stared at her reflection in shocked surprise. "Ha!" Mary thought, "I really do look like a boy!" She laughed aloud. "I bet I can get a job on a snag boat. They will never know I'm not a boy," she said to herself. She laughed and twirled before her reflection, then quietly left town dressed as a boy. She found a ride to the Red River with a family headed there to work on the snag boats.

Several workers had brought their wives and children. This family, the Williams, felt sorry for Mary because she was young and alone. They treated her just like a family member. Arriving at dusk that evening, they found a cedar grove where they pitched their tents within an easy walk of Captain Shreve's camp.

The next morning Mary applied for a job on the *Souvenir*, one of the two snag boats that Henry Shreve brought to Arkansas. She was hired as a general errand boy for $10.00 a month.

Mary was so excited. She could see Captain Shreve looking at the gigantic "raft." She heard him say, "It is the work of centuries." Captain Shreve had been a hero to Mary ever since the first time she read about him in the newspapers. He had proved to be just as impressive in person as in her mind.

Mary ran errands such as bringing water and food to the workers. She often carried small tools and relayed messages to the other crew members. She could see dozens of people lining the riverbanks as the huge snag boats worked.

Mary was so excited to be a part of this important venture that the work seemed easy to her. Captain Shreve ran a clean and respectful crew. The men were kind to her. One major problem was the tendency of workers to get sick with malaria and other "swamp fevers." This was often frustrating to the crew. Sometimes they didn't have enough workers for a particular task. Mary had made friends with many of them. She worried when someone didn't come to work, realizing they were probably sick.

Mary was beginning to feel homesickness as well. She had been on the snag boat about two weeks. She was beginning to miss her mother and father, and she had almost forgotten why she was so mad at her father in the first place. She knew she should write to them, but she kept putting it off. She was sure that they would be angry with her for running away. She didn't know what to do. She would have had more time to write if she had not met a new friend, Bill.

Bill was an errand boy who worked with Mary. He often helped her when work was extremely difficult. He taught her a great deal about the chores she was expected to do. Sometimes they watched the mighty boats bring out the snags and debris from the river. One day they saw a really large snag. The root alone weighed sixty tons. One tree that was brought up was 160 feet long and four feet thick.

Mary and Bill just couldn't believe the size of the debris coming from the river. They knew that this debris was floating down the river into

Louisiana. Sometimes Mary and Bill would see Mr. Shreve in the evenings because he always supervised these floats. He would always wave to them or stop for a little chat. Mary saw Henry Shreve as her hero.

Blasting with dynamite was the most dangerous work. Mary had to make sure she was tucked into a safe place when the large demolition sticks were fired. By July 3, 1833, about four weeks after Mary left Aunt Sally's, the snag boats had cleared many miles of the raft. They had at one time cleared twenty-six miles in twenty-six days. Mary had completely forgotten that by this time her mother and father must know she was not at Aunt Sally's. That was one part of the plan Mary had not thought through.

Actually, Mama and Papa realized that Mary was not with Aunt Sally after only a few days. Papa made a trip to Washington, the Hempstead County seat, to file some legal papers, and he thought he would go by and see if Mary was ready to come home.

Papa was amazed to hear Aunt Sally say Mary had never returned from Marian's! She had sent a letter to Mary at Marian's home, but no answer had been received yet. All she could do was wait. Papa immediately went to see Marian, who assured him that Mary had not been with her.

Papa became frantic. He rushed home and soon all the uncles, aunts, and cousins began a search for Mary. By the end of June they had concluded that Mary had been kidnapped and had disappeared without a trace.

The entire family was deeply upset. Mama cried much of the time. Papa didn't sleep. He barely ate and lost interest in almost everything. On Independence Day, July 4, 1833, Mama asked Papa to take her up to see the clearing of the river.

Papa was deeply mourning the loss of his daughter. He really didn't want to go anywhere, but he finally agreed simply to satisfy his wife. Early the next morning, Papa harnessed the team and prepared the wagon to go to the river. The weather was hot and sticky, and mosquitoes were a menace. The little party started out thinking it would be better to face the mosquitoes than face another lonely day at home.

About noon Mama and Papa arrived at the area where Captain Shreve's men were working. They were amazed at the progress that had been made. Papa smiled sadly when he saw how much faster the river currents were running. How he wished Mary could have been with him today.

The snag boat, *Souvenir*, was just pulling up to the bank when Mama and Papa arrived at the river bank. Mama was looking at the huge snag boat when she saw a young boy walking on the deck. His walk looked familiar.

The boy turned and looked straight at Mama. Just then, a crew member on the shore shouted, "DYNAMITE!" The crew ran for cover. Mary, still looking at her mother, didn't react quickly enough. The huge blast knocked her to the other side of the boat.

Light Draught Snagboat
From *Frank Leslie's Illustrated Newspaper*, 1869

The boat lurched and Mary, who had been unbalanced by the dynamite blast, lost her footing and fell into the water. Her friend Bill grabbed for her arm, but he lost his footing and went into the river as well. Spectators on the riverbanks yelled and waved until the mighty boat stopped.

"MEN OVERBOARD!" yelled the spectators and the boat crew alike.

Several young men from the snag boat jumped overboard to try to save the "boys." Papa dove in along with several other spectators from the riverbanks.

Mama could not shake the uneasy concern cascading through her body. Her entire being was focused on the young boy. In a matter of minutes, they were found. Bill, who was conscious, was unhurt. The smaller boy appeared to be dead. Papa and Bill grabbed the unconscious lad and pulled him to shore. They gently laid the boy on the ground as Mama rushed up through the crowd.

Suddenly the boy coughed and spit out a mouthful of muddy river water. He tried to sit up. As he sat up, he looked into Papa's eyes.

Papa turned white and fainted. Mama ran up just as Papa fell. She looked at the boy and saw what Papa had seen—their daughter, Mary. The hat was gone and the hairpins had been lost to the river. The errand boy was their daughter! Mary sat up and hugged Mama. By this time Papa had recovered, and both parents wept as they held their daughter.

Bill, though still stunned and confused, went to notify Henry Shreve of the accident. When Mr. Shreve found out about Mary's masquerade, he scolded her gently but in the end he said he understood. He knew that the great adventure had been tempting. He ruffled her hair and told her to come back and see him when she could. Bill begged her not to forget him and she promised to write.

Mary felt so terrible because she had worried her parents so much. She apologized over and over, telling them that she meant to send word that she was all right, but the excitement of the job had occupied her time. She begged them to forgive her.

"Mama, Papa, please forgive me. I'm so sorry that I worried you so much. I'll make it up to you some way," Mary pleaded.

"Honey, we were at fault too, we should have realized how much you wanted to see the snag boat operation." Papa said.

"We love you sweetheart. You are safe, that is all that matters." Mama said, holding Mary in her arms.

Papa said, his voice trembling, "Let's go home Mary. We will come back often to visit."

Mary's parents took their daughter home. They had many adventures to hear about once they were home. Mary had spent about four weeks on the river, but there would be 1,976 snags removed and 1,000 trees felled besides the usual channel clearing before the project ended months later. Mary and her Papa saw and enjoyed much of the action as spectators.

With the river opened to boat traffic, land prices would surely rise. Papa began to purchase more land as soon as he could. In the next three years, many immigrants moved into the area. In 1836, Arkansas Territory became a state. Papa and Mama built a new home closer to the river. They were among the first settlers on the land that bordered the cleared channel

As the years passed, the family built a successful business in the little town of Fulton on the now free flowing Red River. The Red River Raft was gone, but its memory would live on in the long history of Arkansas.

Suggested Reading:

Diana Sherwood, "Clearing the Channel—The Steamboat in Arkansas," *Arkansas Historical Quarterly*, III (Spring 1944), pp. 53-62.

Arkansas Civil War Bandits and Outlaws

Jessie's joints were stiff as he awoke from a very awkward sleeping position on the ground. Water dripped slowly down his face as his sleep-blurred vision cleared and he realized he was in the forest with dew dripping from the leaves on to his face. His twin brother Jacob lay next to him, still sleeping.

Jessie moved around on the ground, just enough to ease the stiffness in his joints. He was careful not to make a sound, not even ruffle a leaf as he moved. He was terrified that one of the outlaws would come back and find them.

Jacob rolled over and moaned in his sleep. Jessie rushed over to him and warned,

"Sh-sh Jacob," whispered a terrified Jessie. "Please be quiet! The outlaws might still be around."

Although the bandits had come early the previous morning, both boys were terrified that they might return.

The year was 1864. The boys and their parents had lived near Yellville, Arkansas, near the Missouri border, before Arkansas and ten other Southern states seceded from the Union and the Civil War began. Pa disagreed with secession and went to fight for the North.

Even some of their closest neighbors had shunned them and their entire family had almost become social outcasts, but Pa stood his ground

Ma worried because community opinion was so divided. Some people hated slavery and wanted to fight for the North. Although few people in North Arkansas actually owned slaves themselves, they thought fighting against their own people was traitorous and believed they should stay with the South. When Pa joined the 35th Union Infantry, most of the neighbors stopped speaking to Ma entirely. Ma decided to send the boys to live with their grandmother in the backwoods of Izard County, deep in the recesses of the Arkansas Ozarks. She thought the boys would be better off away from so much dissention.

Grandma was living all alone because Grandpa had gone to war too. He had decided to fight for the South. Mama thought the boys would be safer from the bandits and other outlaws that were beginning to roam the rugged Ozark Mountains.

They were not close to a large town and nobody owned slaves or a huge plantation there either. The closest town to Grandma's was Sylamore and at the time it was only a post office and a few stores.

Jessie shuddered as he thought how wrong his mother had been. At first they had enjoyed their new surroundings. They could hunt and fish all they wanted. The chores were few because Grandma tried to get by with only a small garden and corn patch. The boys seldom worked more than a couple of hours each day.

Jessie remembered working in the vegetable garden with Grandma just the day before. He could still hear her say:

"Grandpa is too old to go traipsing off to war. Mark my words, boys, no good will come of it. States rights is just a lot of foolishness. A law is a law in my opinion no matter where it comes from," Grandma complained.

Jessie agreed but he didn't miss the misty look that appeared in his Grandmother's eyes. Now Jessie knew that she had been right.

He remembered the day before, when he and Jacob had gone to the barn to milk the cow. Everything seemed so normal. They fed the pigs, and then went to Bossy's stall. She was nowhere to be seen.

Jessie said, "Oh, Jacob! Old Bossy went out the back of the barn. I bet we forgot to close the door. We better go catch her or Grandma will have a fit."

The boys trotted down into the woods near the creek, which ran from the huge spring behind the house. Bossy liked to go there to eat the green grass and drink the cool water.

As Jessie and Jacob made their way down into the deep dark woods behind the shed they heard Bossy's bell. They ran toward the sound and grabbed the cow before she could run away again. They were climbing up from the creek when they thought they heard shots. Jessie was holding Bossy's neck rope. He released her and slapped her on the hip, and she ran back into the woods.

"Run, Bossy! Run!" Jessie urged. "Something bad is going on at the house."

The boys slipped closer and closer to the house, creeping silently through the sage grass that grew at irregular intervals. They saw three men riding around on horses in the barnyard shooting into the air, scaring the dogs and cats. Bandits! Two men were in the barnyard chasing the chickens and ringing their necks if and when they caught one. They appeared to be drunk.

A third man was in the barnyard catching the pigs, and trying to cut their throats. He kept sliding down in the mud, and the pigs would slip out of

From: *Harper's Weekly*, 1866

his hands and get away. He killed two or three pigs before a man from inside the house yelled for them to come inside. Jessie and Jacob slipped closer to the house seeking a glimpse of Grandma.

They saw a large red-haired man in the kitchen. They crept closer to the house. The man was shouting at his men. "Hurry up, you lazy fools! We need to get out of here." Then he shouted at Grandma. "Hurry up with that grub," he yelled in a slurred voice.

Jessie and Jacob looked at each other. They knew that they were looking at John Dart. He was one of the most notorious men in the state of Arkansas. Rumor had it that he and his gang lived in a cave and preyed on women and children who lived alone. He was known to be cruel and heartless, always treating his victims badly, especially the women.

He had been known to burn women's faces or their feet and sometimes he even killed them. He often destroyed or vandalized the homes of his victims as well. Terror ran like a hot bolt of lightning through the veins of the teenagers. They looked at each other silently, their eyes widening with great fear. Their grandmother was completely at the mercy of this horrible man.

The boys knew that Dart was there in all his fury. But, they also knew he was drunk. The whiskey would make him even meaner. They could see that Grandmother was trying to hurry, trying to do what she was told but she was shaking so hard she couldn't do anything right. Dart slapped her as hard as he could, telling her to hurry once again.

Grandmother slumped against the kitchen table, shaking so hard her knees barely held her. The men in the other room were yelling and breaking things as she pulled herself up with trembling arms. They were systematically ripping the feather beds to shreds and then pouring molasses on the spilled feathers.

They were making sure that the feathers could never be used again. They also broke the chairs and tables and scattered everything they could find across the floors.

They broke crocks of molasses and honey and then threw the sticky liquids on the floor and windows. Window curtains, towels, and everything they could find was dashed to the floor. Suddenly, Jacob and Jessie heard their Grandmother scream. Dart was slapping her again and again. Screaming that she was an old, useless woman, he slammed his fist into her face. She slumped, and then fell, hitting her head against the table as she went down.

One of the other men yelled, "John, I think she is dead. We better get out of here fast. She had no money anyway."

"Well, go get the meat from the smokehouse and whatever else you can find. We'll make tracks now so we can get back to the cave before dark. Nobody will find us there. We will be safe for a while. James Cotton can look all he wants, but he will never find our cave," Dart bragged. Dart knew that James Cotton would come for him. James Cotton was the United States Army General assigned to this region. His headquarters was located at Yellville. Dart knew that Cotton had no sympathy for him.

The boys watched the men gather up the meat from the smokehouse along with the dried vegetables, onions, potatoes and dried fruit that Grandma had stored for the winter. They watched the outlaws ride away. The boys were shaking, terrified for their grandmother. They looked at the carnage left behind. Three of the pigs were dead. Two had escaped.

Most of the chickens, ducks, and geese were dead, although a few remained. At least the old cow had escaped. The boys were pretty sure they could find her.

The boys carefully eased into the house. Smoke was bellowing from the fireplace. The entire room looked like it was on fire. Grandma had spilled a pan of grease as she hit the floor. The boys quickly doused the flames that were burning the floor. Thank God they got to it in time. Next, they went to check on their grandmother. At first they thought she was dead, but when Jessie touched her, she began to moan and cough. She had inhaled a lot of smoke.

Jessie wiped his grandmother's brow, and she slowly opened her eyes. Thank God she was alive. The boys carried her down to the little shed by the spring. Jacob and Jessie would go back later and look for what little the outlaws had left. They would save what they could, then deal with everything else the next day.

Jacob and Jessie settled their grandmother the best they could on the floor of the shed. Exhausted from her ordeal, she went to sleep as soon as she lay down. They went back to see what the bandits had left. They butchered the slain pigs and carried the meat to the springhouse.

When they returned, their grandmother was asleep and breathing normally. The boys went behind the shed and sat under the giant trees. They were so exhausted they fell to the ground and were soon asleep as well.

Jessie awoke just as the sun began to rise. He went into the shed to check on Grandma.

She was sitting up and seemed fine. Jessie realized he was starving. He knew Grandma and Jacob were hungry too. He awoke Jacob and they went to find Old Bossy. Locating her in the tall grass behind the springhouse, they milked her quickly and went back to prepare breakfast. They cooked fresh pork, gravy and biscuits. They all felt better after eating.

Grandma was better, but the trauma had weakened her, and she was covered with bruises. She was weak and could barely walk for almost a week. Slowly, she began to improve enough to go back to the house. Meanwhile, the boys went home every day and worked on cleaning up the mess the bandits had left behind. They didn't want Grandma to see the house, especially the damaged floors.

Each day they gathered eggs from the few remaining chickens and slowly they all regained their lost strength. The house was looking better too, since the boys had replaced the ruined floor with lumber taken from a barn wall.

They found six hens, three geese, and four ducks still alive. Grandmother said at least it was enough to get started again. A few days after they all returned to the house, Preacher Matthews came riding up. He came in for supper and told them all the community news. He said John Dart's outlaw band had been surrounded and killed somewhere up around Little Red River. General Cotton's troops had surrounded the Dart gang and smoked them out of the cave in which they were hiding. Dart and his gang refused all pleas to surrender.

At this news the little family sighed in relief. Maybe they would be safe for a while, at least until another band formed or this awful war came to an end. They still kept supplies hidden in the shed in the dark woods. It would be a long time before they felt safe again.

One month after the tragedy, the neighbors gathered together and brought them what little supplies they could spare. It was enough to last, if they were careful, until next years crops could be harvested.

Grandma didn't want to move away, so she continued to live in her little home. Ma had come down from Marion County to help. When, the war ended in 1865, Pa and Grandpa returned home. Everybody was proud to see them and they all felt safe again. Pa had lost a leg to the war but Grandpa escaped injury. His 23rd Infantry had seen horrible fighting but Grandpa was plain lucky, Pa said.

Ma and Pa decided to stay on in Izard County so they could help Ma's parents. Pa and Grandpa seemed uncomfortable when they were in the same room. Tension stayed strong between their grandfather and their father although they never actually quarreled. Such differences in political opinions could not be healed completely. In later years the boys pondered the terrible tragedy that swept the nation. They told their children and grand-children of the terrible times they had endured during the Civil War.

Suggested Reading:

Michael B. Dougan, editor, *Confederate Women of Arkansas in the Civil War.* Fayetteville, Ark.: M&M Press, 1993.

Leo Huff, "Guerrillas, Jayhawkers and Bushwhackers in Northern Arkansas During the Civil War," *Arkansas Historical Quarterly*, XXIV (Summer 1965), pp. 127-148.

Bass Reeves:
Great Lawman of the West

D an Stevens sat on his porch in Fort Smith, Arkansas reading the November 19, 1909 issue of the *Muskogee Times Democrat*. He had copies of two other papers, dated January 13, 1910 on his lap as well. Dan sat in his favorite rocker, rocking gently and sadly, as he read the newspapers. Memories flooded his mind.

Dan had just returned from Indian Territory, now the state of Oklahoma. For the past five years he had served as deputy to the superintendent of Indian Affairs for the Creek Nation. Dan had arrived in Fort Smith last night and found the newspapers stacked neatly on his porch. He was sure that some of his family had left them there for him. Dan was thirty-seven years old. He picked up the newspaper and began to read:

Bass Reeves Is A Very Sick Man
(*Muskogee Times Democrat*, November 19, 1909)

Bass Reeves, a deputy United States Marshal in old Indian Territory for thirty-two years, is ill at his home in the Fourth Ward and is not expected to live. Reeves was a deputy under Leo Bennett in the last years of the Federal regime in Oklahoma, and also served under Judge Parker in Fort Smith.

In the early days, when the Indian country was overridden with outlaws, Reeves was sent to arrest criminals who were later tried at Fort Smith. These trips sometimes lasted for months, and Reeves would single-handedly capture bands of men charged with crimes from bootlegging to murder and bring them to Fort Smith. He was paid fees in those days, which sometimes amounted to thousands of dollars for a single trip. For a time, Reeves made a great deal of money. He shot a man he was trying to arrest and was tried for murder.

The fight for his life in the courts was a bitter one, but finally Reeves was acquitted. He was freed, but not until most of his money was gone. The veteran black deputy never quailed in facing any man. He was one of the bravest men this country has ever known. He was considered honest and fearless, and a terror to bootleggers.

Reeves' son shot and killed his own wife and Reeves, enforcing the law, arrested his son. The young man was eventually sent to the penitentiary. While the old man is slowly sinking, Bud Ledbetter, who for years was in the government service with Reeves, is a daily visitor in the Reeves home. Police Judge Walrond, who was United States district attorney while Reeves was an Officer, also calls on the old Negro man.

"While Reeves could neither read or write," said Judge Walrond today, "he had a faculty of knowing what warrants to serve on anyone and never made a mistake." Reeves carried a batch of warrants in his pocket and when his superior officers asked him to produce it, the old man would run through them and never fail to pick out the correct one."

Since Oklahoma statehood, Reeves was given a place on the Muskogee Police Force, but became ill and unable to work. For the past year he has been growing weaker, and has but little time to spend in this world. He is nearly eighty-five years old.

Dan's eyes grew misty as he recalled Uncle Bass. He stood up and walked to the edge of the porch. Images of Bass raced through his mind. He remembered how large Uncle Bass looked to him as a child. He could see in his mind the large six-foot two- inch, two hundred pound deputy walking up these very steps to visit with Dan's grandfather, Charlie. The two older men had been friends for years and Dan grew up sitting at the deputy's feet—always longing to hear of his exciting adventures in Indian Territory. Slowly and sadly, Dan turned his attention to the second newspaper.

Bass Reeves Dead

(Muskogee Phoenix, January 13, 1910)

Bass Reeves, Deputy U. S. Marshal of thirty-two years, is dead. He passed away yesterday afternoon about three o'clock and in a short time, news of his death had reached the Federal court house where the announcement was received in the various offices with comments of regret. The news recalled to the officers and clerks many incidents in the early days of the United States Court here in which the old Negro deputy featured heroically.

Bass Reeves had completed thirty-two years service as Deputy Marshal. At the age of sixty-nine, he gave up that position.

For about two years then he served on the Muskogee Police Force, which position he gave up on account of sickness, from which he never fully recovered. Bright's disease and a complication of ailments together with old age were the cause of his death. He died at the age of eighty-five.

The deceased is survived by his wife and ten children, one of whom, a daughter, Mrs. Alice Spahn, lives in Muskogee. The funeral will be held at noon Friday from the Reeves' home at 816 North Howard Street. Arrangements for the funeral had not been completed last evening.

Tears rolled down Dan's face. This last newspaper was two weeks old. He had missed showing his last respects to his old friend. A smile tugged at Dan's face as he remembered back to his thirteenth birthday. As he entered his teens, Dan felt like he owned the world and could do anything a man could do. One evening he had been out hunting squirrels, bringing five plump gray squirrels home for supper. He burst into the kitchen to show his grandfather the bounty. Bass Reeves was sitting at the kitchen table drinking coffee.

"Hey, young man! What have we got here? Can this old man join you for supper?" Reeves asked smiling.

Dan ran up to Uncle Bass, his arms out, and hugged Bass with all his strength.

"When did you get back Uncle Bass? What happened out there? Did you bring in a lot of men this time for Judge Parker.

"Whoa, Whoa, young fellow," laughed Bass, "one question at a time. Let's first skin the squirrels and fix supper, and then we will have time for the tales. I'm going to spend the night. I'm on my way to pick up two brothers near the Texas border."

After supper, Dan listened to Uncle Bass as he told of flushing out a group of robbers who had fled

Bass Reeves, ca. 1890
Photograph courtesy of:
Butler Center for Arkansas Studies
Central Arkansas Library System

into Indian Territory. He told how he rode into camp on his oldest horse. He was dressed as a cattleman. He spent the night at the campfire. As the men began to drink, their talk became free.

Bass was able to find out where they had hidden the money. The next morning when he started to make the arrest, one of the men shot a hole in the deputy's hat. Another shot bounced off his belt buckle, and his quick reflexes with a gun was all that saved his life.

"Oh! Uncle Bass, can I go with you this trip? I'll be so good. I'm big enough to help you and I will always protect your back," Dan pleaded.

"Not this time son," Bass laughed. "I'm going after a bunch of real desperadoes this trip. They have plundered, murdered, and stolen. They are probably the worst band I've heard of. I came to get your Grandfather to help me this time. Now, go to bed. We will be back in about six weeks. You take care of Grandma. I'll take you fishing when I return, I promise." He ruffled Dan's hair and scooted him off to bed.

The next morning Dan watched as Grandma packed a change of clothes for Grandpa and a small sack of food. Hoping to keep their identities secret, the two men dressed as wandering tramps. Dan watched as the two friends rode out of sight.

Dan returned to the house walking slowly, looking forward to the stories his Grandpa and Uncle Bass would tell him when they returned. Grandpa and Uncle Bass returned about a month later. Dan saw them coming up the road. He ran to greet them as they rode up to the house. Grandpa gave Dan a mighty hug.

"Tell me what happened Grandpa; you too, Uncle Bass," Dan begged.

"After supper, son. We are starving for some of your Grandma's good cooking," Grandpa chuckled.

After supper, Uncle Bass and Grandfather sat with Dan on the front porch. Grandpa began to describe their adventures in Indian Territory. He told the tale just like he was reporting it to a newspaper. He told of how Reeves set up a camp several miles from where he suspected the outlaws had their hide out. Bass wanted to study the terrain and take his time planning the capture of the dangerous brothers. Dan's grandfather, Charlie, hid himself in the dense brush close to the camp.

"Bass disguised himself well," Grandpa recalled. "He wore old pants that had been patched in many places. He hid his handcuffs, pistol, and badge under his clothes; and wore an old and badly stained hat. He left his horse behind. I followed behind him, keeping hidden at all times. Bass found the home of the outlaw's mother. She gladly fed him and they discussed her two outlaw sons. When Bass finished eating he told her he was really tired and asked to spend the night."

"She agreed and even said he should join up with her boys," Grandpa said with a twinkle in his eye.

"I waited for the two outlaws to come home. I heard a whistle from the nearby woods. The mother went outside and lit a match for a signal. The outlaws came out of hiding and talked to their mother for quite a while. Bass remained in the house. I wondered if he had fallen asleep," Grandpa recounted.

"Finally," Grandpa continued, "the outlaws went into the house. I crawled up to the shack and peeked into the window. The woman introduced her sons to Bass. The boys agreed to bring Bass into their gang, they all drank heartily from a brown jug of whiskey, and then they stretched out on the floor near the fireplace. Soon they were snoring loudly."

"Bass waited until the outlaws were asleep. He left his bed and silently handcuffed them without awaking either. Then he went back to sleep himself. I watched this with amazement," Grandpa recalled. "I had not slept a wink and didn't expect too, but I nodded off in the hours just before dawn. I was awakened by the commotion coming from the house when the outlaws realized they were in the hands of the law."

"We began the long journey back to Fort Smith with the prisoners. Their mother followed us for more than a mile, cursing and screaming, calling Bass every vile name she knew. Bass told the outlaws they had to walk the long distance to his camp. I had come out of hiding just as Bass made the arrest, but still followed out of sight in the woods in case of a surprise attack," Grandpa concluded.

"Golly, Grandpa and Uncle Bass," Dan remarked, "I want to be a lawman some day and bring in outlaws like you do."

Grandpa and Bass Reeves looked at each other and laughed. They patted Dan on the head and sent him off to bed.

Dan smiled as he remembered those long ago days. He knew he would never know another man with the strength of character of Bass Reeves. Dan worked for the law himself for a few years before he left for Indian Territory. He would never forget the firm but gentle man whose integrity was an example for everyone who knew him.

Suggested Reading:

Art T. Burton, *Black, Red, & Deadly: Black and Indian Gunfighters of the Indian Territory, 1870-1907.* Austin, TX: Eakin Press, 1991.

Nudie E. Williams, "Bass Reeves: Lawman in the Western Ozarks," *Negro History Bulletin*, XLII (April-June 1979), pp. 37-39.

The 1927 Flood

Jake Wilson sat at his desk in a one-room schoolhouse at Palarm, Arkansas. He was nervous; his hands were sweaty, and he was filled with dread.

Jake was doing his oral report on the great flood that raged through the Palarm community and much of the rest of Arkansas in 1927. Although this disaster happened five years earlier, when Jake was eight years old, he had not forgotten the horrible event. He still had a stiff leg due to an injury he received while stranded in the floodwaters.

"Jake," Mrs. Kelly called out, "it is time for your report."

Jake walked up to the podium and looked out over the classroom. His leg was hurting today, his limp was more pronounced than usual. He knew this was because he was nervous. As he looked at his classmates, he realized that every one of them had suffered some kind of loss because of this flood. Some had lost much more than he. They, like Jake and his family, were still trying to rebuild their lives. Some had lost their homes or livestock or both. Mandy Sue had lost her younger cousin. Mrs. Kelly, the teacher, had lost her husband of two months.

Jake and his family lost all their cattle and their home. Jake had been injured too, but his injury wasn't severe enough to prevent him from leading a normal life. He was very thankful for that.

He looked at his audience and with a deep breath began:

"Mrs. Kelly and classmates. I am going to report on the Great Flood of 1927. I realize this report will touch the hearts and minds of everybody here.

"The Flood began in February of 1927. The worst flooding was in the Delta part of Arkansas. But, we were hit hard too here in central Arkansas.

"The Flood was huge, covering parts of seven states in the Mississippi River Valley. Nearly 800,000 people were forced to flee their homes. Many were rescued from housetops, trees, levees, or railway embankments.This flood started from rains that fell for months over thirty-one states and two Canadian provinces. These rains drained southward into an area of 1,240,000 square miles. Some of this water evaporated or soaked into the ground but most of it slowly made its way down the Mississippi River to the Gulf of Mexico.

"The Arkansas River, a major tributary of the Mississippi also flooded. By the time the floodwaters reached central Arkansas, the Arkansas River was a foul and swirling sea.

"The yellow waters came rushing and swirling through Palarm, a small community located on the Arkansas River near the Pulaski-Faulkner County lines. The river carried in its dark tide the remains of animals, trees, trash, fences, bridges, houses, barns, and chicken coops that had been collected by fifty-four flooded tributaries. This refuse literally changed the color of the waters.

"Levees broke and farms were flooded. The swollen carcasses of mules, hogs, horses and cows glutted the bayous. Buzzards fed on the dead animals. Everywhere, rescue boats churned the yellow tide, hauling hundreds of silent, dazed people to safer places."

Jake stopped to clear his throat. His classmates sat silently. Everyone was taken back to the tragic events of five years ago.

Jake remembered the cold flood waters and the deaths of livestock.

He turned back to the class and continued to speak:

"Steel bridges collapsed and railroad boxcars floated freely. Ruined sawmills and cotton gins were common everywhere. Thousands of survivors were trapped on the levees or in second story houses, or barn lofts.

"In April 1927, the Red Cross organized a huge rescue force consisting of a mobile fleet, ranging from Navy tugboats to commandeered steamers, barges and fishing craft. The bigger boats continued to work at night, crashing over tops of submerged trees, dodging floating houses or even venturing onto village streets. They flashed huge searchlights into the night, seeking out people, often finding them perched on anything they could find above the swirling waters.

"Sometimes the boats came too late. One man, after realizing that his house was floating away, got his wife and children out of a bedroom window and up into a tree. He barely had the strength to pull himself up from the rising water to join his family. When the rescue boats arrived at dawn, they found the man alone, his family washed away during the night.

"But, on a lighter note, of all the animals caught in the flood, the mule remained alert and curious. My dad described the actions of one of his mules.

"He said his mule would watch the roaring airplanes with ears pointing this way and that, snorting now and then to show his astonishment at the large creatures that flew above his head. He would paw the ground and snort at the high-powered surfboats scooting by. Tired cows simply bawled, but the mule gazed steadily around waiting anxiously to see what would happen next. Every house was searched for people and animals. If a house had been searched, a red flag was nailed to it. One evening a boat passed a house with a red flag nailed on it. They heard shrill cries that sounded like a woman in deep distress. As they neared the house, they were astonished to see the heads of four panthers at an attic window, screaming loudly as if crying for help.

"Most of the refugees came into camp wet, weak, and despondent. Many had lost everything except the clothes on their backs. But, usually a nights rest on a dry bed and a good breakfast restored their courage and spirits.

"After the rescues were made and the waters went down, the big job was to put half a million people back on the land, provide housing, furniture, bedding, food, seeds, implements, and animals to work with. The farm animals that survived were distributed almost at random. It was a pitiful struggle. From all over America, people sent food and clothing. Railroads transported these items for free.

"Texas sent a trainload of buses and automobiles to help people. Ford Motor Company rushed hundreds of lifeboats to the Red Cross. In Arkansas alone, fifty thousand dead animals had to be buried or burned in the flooded areas.

"Drinking water was contaminated. Flies and mosquitoes bred by the billions. People of every community worked until they literally dropped in their tracks, building levees higher with sandbags, pushing wheelbarrow loads of soil trying to contain the water.

"Many people called this flood the 'Great American Sewer' because

South Bend, Arkansas During the 1927 Flood
Photograph courtesy of:
Butler Center for Arkansas Studies
Central Arkansas Library System

of the yellow contaminated body of water, colored by the offal of thousands of dead animals and uprooted timber often "backed up" into its tributaries. These tributaries were rivers such as the Arkansas River, the Red River, the Black River and the St. Francis River.

"As long as the waters of the tributaries stayed higher than the Mississippi, they flowed into it fine. But when the Mississippi flooded, its waters were higher and the swollen mess backed up into the rivers feeding into it." Jake stopped again. He took a drink from the water glass one more time. He gazed at his classmates who were shifting uncomfortably in their seats. He could feel their empathy. He could see by the sadness in their faces that they also remembered this terrible time. He cleared his throat, then continued:

"The statistics of the flood in Arkansas show that Pulaski County covers a total of 779 square miles. The Arkansas River cuts diagonally across it from Northwest to Southeast. This county is the most thickly settled area in the state.

"The county's 1927 population was estimated at 155,000 people. The Red Cross gave substantial help to 3,557 families. This included housing, clothing, farm animals, and medical supplies. There are no accurate statistics of those who received temporary relief. Temporary relief was given to almost everybody in some form."

Finished at last, Jake walked to his seat. Mrs. Kelly paused for a moment, still lost in her own thoughts.

"Jake, that was a wonderful report. It shows us that we can overcome all odds if we stay together and help each other. We all remember the flood for our own special reasons." Mrs. Kelly sighed.

"Yes ma'am, Mrs. Kelly," Jake said. "I remember it well. I was the last one of the children in my family to be rescued by Pa's old mule, Ned. We were lucky that our family was saved but we lost all our possessions.

Jake continued, "My leg was broken by a huge tree caught up in the currents rushing by our house. It was hours before my rescue. I'll never walk completely right again. But, at least I can walk; many people suffered much more. I can do about anything I want to. I'm grateful for that ma'am. We still have that old mule. He is retired now. He is just my pet."

Mrs. Kelly smiled gently but sadly. She said, "Thank you Jake." She continued, "The flood of 1927 was a terrible economic event for our state. The crash of the stock market in 1929 also hurt the economy. The drought of 1930 and the Great Depression that caused cotton prices to drop drastically in 1931 put our economy in turmoil. We have had five years of one economic tragedy after the other. We have had to face many challenges in the last five years. I believe they have made us strong enough to face the challenges of the future."

"It is time to go home, class. I'm looking forward to the oral reports tomorrow. Today has been an educational and emotional day," she said.

The teacher watched as the students quickly walked from the classroom. She hoped they would never take anything for granted again. Mrs. Kelly started walking toward home, grateful that her four-year old son would be waiting there for her, anxious to run into his mother's arms. Mrs. Kelly sighed, and then smiled as her steps became faster and she hurried home to her son.

Suggested Reading:

John M. Barry, *Rising Tide: The Great Mississippi Flood of 1927 and How It Changed America.* New York: Simon & Schuster, 1997.

Frederick Simpich, "The Great Mississippi Flood of 1927," *National Geographic Magazine*, LII (September 1927), pp. 243-289.

Sunburns and Sore Muscles... Working to Save the Farm During the Great Depression

Charlene was picking cotton in a field near Blytheville, Arkansas. The late August sun was beating down on her back and the wind almost blistered the very earth itself. The air was heavy with the smell of the swamp that bordered the cotton field. The year was 1935.

Charlene dragged the heavy cotton sack up one long dusty row and down the next. The strap on the canvas sack pressed deeply into her shoulder and back, resulting in a continuing ache. She knew she would ache even more before nightfall.

The heavy white bolls of cotton bent the plants almost to the ground. The soil was dry and dusty, which was not unusual during the early autumn cotton picking season.

Charlene looked up toward the shimmering red sun. Not having a watch, she guessed it was around three o'clock in the afternoon. Her scanty lunch, which had consisted of fried potatoes in a biscuit sandwich, vanished long ago. She longed to take off her cotton sack and go to the cabin and rest.

Charlene rubbed her index finger where a green cotton boll had pricked her skin. Tears came to her eyes as the stinging sensation throbbed. She was very tired. All she wanted was to go to the cabin to eat and rest. As she thought of the cabin, she shuddered as she recalled the old plank walls and floor. Large cracks appeared between most boards. Even the knotholes were falling out! Rusty tin roofing clung precariously to the sagging rafters. It seemed that the tin roof actually glowed under the hot August sun.

The cabin consisted of one large room with a little "lean to" shed on the side. Charlene's two brothers slept on two old mattresses on the floor in the tiny shed. A fireplace hugged the wall of the large room. Ma had converted this room into a kitchen and two tiny sleeping areas. Ma had an old kerosene cooking stove in the far corner of the big room. Dishes and canned goods were crammed into wooden crates and boxes that substituted for kitchen cabinets.

An old hand-powered water pump sat in the other corner, with a rusty round tub set under it. Pa had an old rocking chair that sat beside the fireplace. He loved to listen to the news and the Grand Ole Opry on a battery-powered radio. Like most homes in Mississippi County, Arkansas in 1935, this house had no electricity.

Ma had divided the rest of the big room with sheets to provide a sleeping area for Charlene and her sisters, Carrie and Leah. Ma and Pa had the other "bedroom." They, too, slept on old mattresses brought from home. Their few clothes hung limply from nails along the walls.

Charlene shuddered as she thought of the old gnarled Cypress tree that grew in the back yard. Its roots were large and curled up through the ground like a giant serpent. The limbs were twisted and the trunk looked like a broken-down old man. Charlene was fourteen years old, but the old tree gave her the shivers every time she walked near it. It seemed almost alive.

Charlene quickly checked herself. She berated herself for sinking into self-pity. She and her family should be very thankful for the work. At least now Pa might have a chance to save the family farm in North Arkansas.

She looked at her brothers and sisters who were laboring close by. Her mother and father worked side by side just like the whole family. Her sister, Carrie, looked at her and winked, although, her face was blistered red by the unrelenting sun.

Charlene loved her brothers and sisters. She was the youngest in a family of five children. She and her brother, John, looked like Ma. They had dark hair, almost black eyes, and a dark complexion. Carrie, Leah and Curt were lighter. They had green eyes and sandy brown hair, the same as their father. The family had always been close. Charlene's sister, Carrie, was sixteen, John was eighteen, Curt was twenty, and Leah was twenty-one. Aunt Mendy called them "stair steps." So far, the older children had not married but Charlene thought that would change once they had saved the family farm.

Charlene sighed as she straightened her back and waved to her sister Leah. She realized that this arduous work was necessary because the economy had failed all over the world. Pa could not sell his corn, cattle or hogs for enough money to pay the mortgage and supply their basic needs.

Charlene remembered last year just before her school closed for the season. Her teacher, Mr. Clark, had told the class that bitter days were ahead.

Mr. Clark had said that a great depression hit the United States in October of 1929. He said this marked the beginning of the greatest economic disaster in history. He said unwise borrowing, the economic problems caused by World War I, poor banking practices, and the terrible general poverty among farmers and factory workers had all led to this disaster. Many Arkansas farmers had lost their homes. Some had moved to Oregon and California to try to start over.

Charlene didn't understand much about the economic impact of a huge war or even the economic conditions of the state of Arkansas, but she knew Pa could no longer pay the bank loan. His calves and pigs brought very little when sold and the government was telling them to raise huge gardens and plant peas instead of corn. The Federal government had even passed out pressure cookers with jars, cans, and instructions on how to preserve food so people would not starve.

Charlene stopped picking cotton for just a minute. She moved the heavy cotton sack to the other shoulder. She walked back to the end of the

Cotton Pickers, Oil Trough, Arkansas, ca. 1910

cotton row where the water jug sat under a tall oak tree. She drank deeply as her thoughts turned to the day her best friend Sally told her that the bank had foreclosed on her family's farm. Sally wept as she told Charlene that her family was leaving Arkansas to look for work. Her dad thought he could find work in the lumber mills of Oregon or northern California.

Sadly, Charlene ran home, splashing through the creek below her house. She only waved at Old Blue, her pony, as she passed him and ran into the house. Her mother and sisters were in the kitchen canning with the new pressure cooker. Ma had canned corn, potatoes, tomatoes, green beans, mustard greens, beet pickles, cucumber pickles, turnips and turnip greens, peas, okra, and every other garden vegetable they could raise in the garden patches near the creek.

Ma had even canned all of the young chickens that had hatched off in the spring, along with all the old hens that no longer laid eggs. Now, Charlene ran crying into her mother's arms. She told her mother that Sally's family was moving to Oregon or California. Her heart was breaking at the loss of her friend.

Shaken, she sobbed, "Ma what if we have to leave? What would we do with Old Blue and all the other animals? Ma! I'm so scared. What if we lose our farm?"

Charlene's mother held her gently, tenderly rocking her in her arms.

"Honey it might not be so bad for us." she said. "We have canned a great deal including meat this year. Pa thinks he might get us a job in Blytheville working for my cousin's husband. He has gone to town to call him right now. If we work hard at this job, and take most of our food with us, we might be able to make the loan payment on the farm after all."

Her mother reassured her, "next year Pa might get to work on the WPA, a program developed by newly elected President Franklin D. Roosevelt. Uncle Zed said that people up here might be working for the government by next year. He said our new President promised jobs for many people in Arkansas. Maybe this job will help us to hold out until then."

Charlene dried her tears and began to help Carrie set the table for supper. With a loud whoop, Pa came in just as Ma set a pan of hot cornbread on the table . Smiling broadly, he grabbed Ma around the waist and danced her around the kitchen.

"We got the job, honey." Pa shouted. "Henry Jakes said he would use our whole family. He thinks we might be able to work at least two months."

"Pa," Charlene ventured.

"What honey?" he answered.

"Pa, uh, uh ……..what kind of work will we be doing?"

Pa walked over to the kitchen table and sat down. He looked at the food, then back at Ma. He squared his shoulders and sat up as straight as he could. He looked at his family and smiled.

"Well, honey we will be picking cotton."

The children grew very quiet. They had never picked cotton, but they had hoed corn, fed the cattle, hogs and chickens. They had hauled hay, shelled corn, and cut and split firewood. But they had no concept of how difficult it was to pick cotton all day. They looked at each other and smiled. They could do it! They could do whatever it took to save the farm. They just couldn't lose it now.

Charlene's daydreaming ended quickly as a green cotton boll sailed over her head barely missing her.

She whirled around just as her brother John yelled, "Charlene what are you daydreaming about? It is time to go to the cabin for supper."

Charlene was relieved. She dragged the full cotton sack behind her up to the huge trailer that held the cotton. The owner of the cotton fields weighed each bag and paid each according to the number of pounds picked. Cotton was picked for about fifty cents per hundred pounds. If Charlene picked two hundred pounds of cotton in one day, she would make one dollar. But, Charlene had two brothers and two sisters and Ma and Pa too. The two brothers and Pa could each pick about three hundred pounds of cotton every day.

Ma could pick around two hundred and fifty pounds and the older girls could pick about the same. The family worked six days a week. The whole family made about fifty-five dollars each week.

They spent about ten dollars a week for groceries, including milk and kerosene to fuel their lamp, because they brought much of their food with them. If they could save even thirty dollars a week, Pa said they could pay the mortgage for this year and buy coffee, flour, sugar, and tea for the next year. This sounded good to Charlene.

They often walked from the cotton fields back home with a black family that was picking cotton too. They talked and joked as they walked. Charlene especially liked Belle, one of the girls close to her age. They often picked cotton together and talked and sang to pass the days.

When they returned to the cabin, Ma opened a jar of canned chicken, then she made biscuits and gravy. The children took a quick sponge bath and sat down to eat.

Pa collected the picking money from each family member. Pa counted silently, and then announced, "We made $9.25 today. This has been a good day."

As soon as the dishes were washed, Pa and Ma sat down on the corner of the bed and sang and played a few songs on their guitars. Charlene went to sleep as she heard Pa whisper to Ma that he would be back shortly. He wanted to hunt a little around the swamp. Charlene knew that meant frog legs for tomorrow's supper. Ma cautioned him to be careful as she began washing the clothes they had worn that day.

The next thing Charlene knew it was morning again. Charlene and Belle were working close together as usual. Charlene heard Belle scream.

"Charlene! There is a giant bug on the cotton stalk. I don't know what it is. Come see."

Charlene ran to her friend. "Oh! Belle, it is just a large spider. Don't scare it and it will go away."

Sure enough the spider went away and the girls laughed about the "giant bug" the rest of the day.

The days and nights dragged on the same for the next three weeks. The work was hard. And every day seemed longer than the day before. The sun seemed to get hotter and hotter. Pa said he didn't believe the work would last more than six weeks, maybe not even that. Ma said she would try to stretch-out the food. She began to make peas into patties for the family to take to the fields.

The peas looked good, just like sausage cakes, but still tasted like peas. Charlene could hardly eat them anymore unless she was really hungry. She knew she would never like black-eyed peas again. She longed for the fresh fish they caught back home.

Ma also cooked frog legs, squirrels, raccoon, and fish to supplement the meals. Pa's swamp hunting and river trips really helped. Sometimes he would get a few crawfish and eels from the river. That was always a treat. He would take the whole family and they, too, would fish. Ma often prepared a picnic lunch and the children enjoyed a swim.

Exactly eight weeks and two days after they arrived, the last cotton was picked. Pa and Ma sat around the homemade kitchen table counting their money carefully. They were counting every single coin, even the pennies. Finally, Pa sighed with relief.

He said, "We have saved two hundred and twenty dollars. Our mortgage payment on the farm is one hundred and twenty-five dollars and forty cents for the year, including interest." He concluded hopefully, "I think we can make our payment and have enough money left for living expenses for the remainder of the year."

Ma sighed! "Oh heavens! I am so relieved. For a while I really was afraid we wouldn't be able to make it."

Everybody hugged. Charlene quietly left the festivities and walked out on the porch of the old shack. She knew she would miss Belle but she was ready to go home. She couldn't wait to get back to the green fields and beautiful sparkling brook of the farm. Tomorrow they would pack up the old pickup and head home. Charlene knew that many problems would face their family in the near future. The economy was far from good and she suspected this would be true for years to come.

She hoped her brothers would not be forced to leave home to find work as had happened to so many other families back home. She walked slowly back into the shack. She hoped with her whole heart that they could continue to overcome the great crisis, which would become known as the Great Depression.

Suggested Reading:

Grubbs, Donald H. *Cry from the Cotton: The Southern Tenant Farmers' Union and the New Deal.* Chapel Hill: The University of North Carolina Press, 1971.

The WPA Guide to 1930s Arkansas. Introduction by Elliott West. Lawrence: University Press of Kansas, Lawrence. 1987.

Timber: Living and Working in an Arkansas Forest

E ddie woke up excited. Today was moving day again. Eddie's father, John Drake, worked on a logging crew for the Caddo River Lumber Company. John was a hauler; which meant he had to move frequently from one logging camp to another. The camps where the loggers lived moved as soon as all the timber was cut from the area.

John was beginning a new job in the Ouachita Mountains, which covered much of western Arkansas, including most of Montgomery County where the family lived. John was very proud of his job, especially since they were in a depression and jobs were hard to find. This new year of 1933 promised to be a better year for John and his family. He had been logging for twelve years, ever since Eddie was born, but he began hauling logs only six months earlier. The Arkansas flood of 1927 along with many droughts as well as the fall of Wall Street in 1929 had hurt the economy everywhere, especially in an underdeveloped state like Arkansas.

These economic tragedies had even hurt the logging industry. John was very lucky indeed. Many people in Arkansas had lost their homes and were moving out of state to find work.

Eddie hurried into the house to eat breakfast. Mom was in a rush, as always, on moving day. Eddie's house belonged to the Caddo River Lumber Company. As a matter of fact, every house that the loggers occupied belonged to the Company, which was owned by T.W. Rosborough.

Mr. Rosborough provided portable houses that could be moved from one campsite to the other on flatcars pulled by locomotives, which let the loggers take their homes and families with them to each new work site.

Eddie's house was small. It measured twelve by twenty four feet and had two rooms. The large room had a cook stove and served as a kitchen, dining room and a sitting room. Eddie and his brother Ben also slept in the sitting room on a bed that served as a couch when they had visitors. The other room was much smaller and served as a bedroom for Eddie's parents. It held a bed, and a dresser with a mirror. The dresser held the family valuables.

The larger room also contained a rocking chair, and a wood heating stove. Most of the family's clothes were hung on various nails on the walls.

The camp house was built with unpainted board-and-batten exteriors, which meant small boards about an inch wide were nailed over the cracks of the larger boards. The inside walls were covered with a decorate wall paper. With a wood fire blazing in the metal stove, these houses were actually quite warm and comfortable. Eddie and Ben loved living in the portable house.

"Eddie, finish your breakfast as soon as you can," admonished his mother. "We must get out of here as soon as possible so the snipes can get our house loaded onto the railroad flatcar." The "snipes" were men who moved the houses onto railroad flat cars.

Eddie ate hurriedly, not taking time to butter his biscuit and gulping his bacon and eggs. After handing his plate to his mother, he hurried outside to wait for the snipes. As he waited, Eddie remembered the previous night. He and his brother, Ben, had taken his mother's chickens off the roost. They put them in a portable coop that Dad had made long ago. They would load it on to the locomotive with the house to take to the new camp.

Fourteen-year-old Ben, was helping his dad and Uncle Paul take down the tall cabinets and stovepipes. They were also removing the legs from the wood burning stoves. Eddie's job had been to watch for the snipes and run errands for mother and Aunt Sue as they finished the last minute packing for the movers. Finally, Dad and Ben took the mirrors off the dressers and laid them on the beds.

They pushed the beds and stoves to the side of the house. Mom and Uncle Paul's wife, Aunt Sue, were busy tying the furniture to the nails on the walls. This was to keep the furniture from moving and sliding, maybe even breaking during the move. They removed the pictures from the walls, often calling for Eddie to do some small chore as he watched for the moving men.

Mom and Aunt Sue hurriedly packed their dishes in washtubs filled with cushioning straw; they carefully stored the kerosene lamps to protect their fragile glass chimneys.

"Eddie! Hurry and hand me another quilt to wrap around the lamps," Aunt Sue called.

Eddie sighed, amazed at how fast everybody was working. He looked up and saw the snipes approaching. The two men had gone into the woods and cut two pine trees to serve as skid poles. They dragged the skid poles into camp with a pair of mules.

Meanwhile the train's crew positioned a flatcar beside Eddie's house. They uncoupled the locomotive engine from the car while the snipes pulled two cables and hooked them to the floor sills. Then they fastened these lines to another cable which was then pulled across the flatcar, through a pulley tied to a tree and down the tracks to the locomotive, where they fastened the cable to the back of the engine. The engine would then gently move forward as the house was pulled up the skid poles on to the flatcar.

Awestruck, Eddie watched all this activity. Ben had come to join him by now. Dad and Mom were loading the last items into the log wagon. The family milk cow was tied securely to the back of the wagon. Eddie ran up to his dad with a pleading expression in his eyes.

"Dad! Please let us wait here and watch them put the house on the flatcar," he begged. "Ben and I could ride up to the new campsite with the house and the chickens. We hardly ever stay behind to watch them load the house. Please, just this one time Dad!"

Dad looked at Mom. They smiled. "Well, I guess this one time we can let you watch them and ride up on the train." Dad smiled. "Mom and I will go on ahead so we can be ready to set up once the house is unloaded."

Eddie excitedly ran back to tell Ben. "Ben! Dad and Mom are going to let us stay and watch the snipes load the house onto the flatcar and ride the train to the new campsite." Eddie shouted, jumping with excitement.

"Yeah, Eddie. It will be fun riding the train." Ben smiled, slapping Eddie on the shoulder.

A Southern Logging Camp, ca. 1910

Eddie's attention was quickly drawn from his brother as he watched two men finish peeling bark from the two skid poles. Once the bark had been removed, one end of each pole was placed under the edge of the house while the other ends were placed on the flatcar, providing a ramp so the house could be winched on to the flatcar.

The section boss looked at the boys and waved. "Be careful now, and stay out of our way in case this skid pole should slip. We wouldn't want you to get hurt, now would we?" he said, frowning.

Eddie and Ben nodded and stepped back several feet. Eddie watched the man who had cautioned him pick up a grease bucket and brush the skid poles. This would help the house slide up the poles with greater ease.

When the poles were slippery enough, the snipe raised a hand into the air, signaling the engineer to begin the loading. Slowly the locomotive moved forward, pulling the cable tight. With a mighty jerk, the house began to slide up the poles, all the while shuddering and swaying. Inch-by-inch the small house moved up the skid poles.

Suddenly, a great snapping sound split the air. Eddie and Ben cringed as they saw the huge cable snap and sail away from the locomotive. The long piece of steel cable flew through the air at a frightening speed. It cut through the pathway exactly where Ben and Eddie had been standing, wrapped itself around a couple of trees, and dropped to the ground.

"Are you alright?" shouted one of the snipes.

"Yes," the boys shouted in unison, their voices shrill with excitement and some fear.

"We were all very lucky," said the snipe. "Someone could have been killed if they had been in the path of that cable."

"Do you think you can get the house on the train now?" asked Ben

"Yes, son, it just slipped. We can draw it back tight and tie it off. Everything will be okay." He smiled over his shoulder as he walked away.

Eddie and Ben watched as the crew re-threaded the cable. Soon the house was swaying and shuddering up the poles again. Finally, it balanced over onto the deck of the flatcar, and was securely tied in place. Everybody sighed with relief, and the train began to move slowly.

Eddie and Ben jumped on to the flatcar as it slowly passed by. They sat on the flatcar beside the house and watched the scenery.

They saw beautiful forest birds of many kinds and colors, such as cardinals and blue jays and beautiful yellow and brown birds that they could not identify. They saw a herd of deer drinking from a sparkling pool, their antlers shimmering with the morning dew. The boys smiled as the deer sprinted away into the forest as the train approached.

"Look Eddie!" Ben gasped. "That is more deer than I have seen in many months. They are so beautiful this time of year."

Eddie nodded and smiled. His attention was totally captured by the beautiful, graceful animals of the forest. The train ride was full of wonder as they gazed at wild ducks and beautiful water birds of every type.

They even spotted some wild geese flying overhead but they could not make up their minds as to what direction the birds were headed. The boys loved the train ride and they decided to come back and fish in the beautiful pool where they had seen the deer drinking. Maybe Mom and Dad would come also and they could all have a picnic lunch.

When they reached their new camp they went to find their parents. They could not wait to share the adventures of their day. They found their parents near a huge spring flowing from a crevice in a small cliff. This water fell into a small pool that flowed into a narrow brook that slowly meandered through the forest.

Mom and Dad had decided this was the place to set their house. Mom could get water easily here. The boys turned loose the cow in tall grass near the water where she could eat contentedly, assuring the family plenty of milk. The section crew had already cleared spaces for the houses while the train was arriving. They were using two teams of mules to pull the houses off the flatcars.

By late that afternoon the snipes had all the houses set up again and Eddie and Ben were put to work unpacking everything and finding a place to set the portable chicken coop.

The men of the family, meanwhile, assembled the stovepipes so Mom and Aunt Sue could begin cooking supper. Everyone was hungry and could hardly wait. Dad was complaining that everything had been "sprung" out of shape and nothing would fit anymore.

Mom was talking to dad, gently reassuring him that everything would look better after he ate a good hot meal. She was sure right! Everything did seem better after supper. By bedtime, all the furniture was in place and everything looked just like home again. The boys were delighted to crawl into bed after such a busy and exciting moving day.

Dad and Mom sat at the kitchen table drinking coffee and talking. Mom was planning to raise a huge garden to help with the food bills. The Company commissary or grocery store was owned by the logging company and was very expensive. Mom was always looking for ways to save money. Dad's wages were paid by the board foot that he hauled. He was usually paid $1.45 per thousand board feet for short hauls up to one-fourth mile and $1.65 for one-fourth to one half mile hauls.

Dad thought he could make more money doing the short hauls. He thought he might make between four and five dollars a day. This was good money during the 1930s. Eddie could hear his parents talking. He jumped out of bed to ask his Dad a question.

"Dad," asked Eddie, "What exactly is a board foot?"

"Well, Eddie," his father said, "a board foot is equal to a board measuring twelve inches long, twelve inches wide, and one inch thick. So, son, I have to haul the equivalent of one thousand boards that measure 12 inches long, by 12 inches wide, by one inch thick for one-fourth of a mile to earn $1.45. So, I have to haul a lot of trees to earn $5.00 per day.

"Boy, Dad, you really work hard to make a living don't you," Eddie sighed.

"I don't mind, son. It's my job to make a living for my family. I would not be happy any other way. I love to work with the timber and the forest. And it sure beats trying to grow cotton on these rocky hillsides."

"Thanks dad," Eddie sighed as he hugged his father and went back to bed.

Eddie fell asleep thinking that logging must be the best job in the world in order for his dad to enjoy it so much.

It seemed but a minute when Mom awoke the boys for breakfast. They ate hurriedly and began the walk to a farm Mom and Dad had passed yesterday on the way to camp. Here, Mom could buy food supplies cheaper than at the commissary. Eddie was happy. He could hear the huge saws running.

Suggested Reading:

Kenneth L. Smith, *Sawmill: The Story of Cutting the Last Great Virgin Forest East of the Rockies*. Fayetteville: University of Arkansas Press, 1986.

Japanese Americans and The Rohwer Relocation Camp

N orico Murahani was fifteen years old. She was a California girl. She considered her parents somewhat old fashioned because they still clung to some of the old Japanese ways. Today, April 10, 1967, Norico was especially agitated. Mom had announced last night that Uncle Tomo was coming to Los Angeles from San Francisco for a family visit. Norico's parents and Uncle Tomo, along with several other families, planned to make a trip to Arkansas to visit the site of the old Rohwer Relocation Camp.

Norico could not imagine why they would want to go to a far-away state such as Arkansas and relive all those painful memories that make all the older people so sad. She wished they would forget the whole thing. Now, they were going to drag her along and she would have to listen to the old stories for a week or so. How boring, she thought.

Norico picked up the phone to call her friend Shelia. Shelia was a Native American and Norico's best friend. Her people also had a tragic past. The girls were more interested in the present than the past, and they both wished their families would forget about all the wrongs of the past.

Now, Uncle Tomo and her parents were going to drag her to some distant state her friends barely knew existed.

Shelia didn't answer the phone. Norico went to help her mother with supper, still fuming at the situation.

Just then Dad arrived with Uncle Tomo. After Uncle Tomo was comfortably settled and dinner was completed, the family moved to the living room where discussions continued over coffee. They discussed the old days just as Norico feared. Finally, Norico was allowed to go to bed. She sighed in relief as she walked into her room and closed the door.

The next day, three families left for Arkansas in two cars. The trip was uneventful and boring to Norico. She stared out the window, wishing with all her heart that she was back in California.

They arrived in Arkansas two days later. They went to their hotel rooms and dressed for dinner. After dinner the extended family gathered in a hotel room and continued to discuss the unfortunate experiences during World War II.

Uncle Tomo and Norico's grandparents were among the 120,000 Japanese Americans who were forced into camps by the United States Army after the Japanese attack at Pearl Harbor on December 7, 1941. Uncle Tomo's family was sent to Rohwer, a relocation camp near McGehee, in Southeast Arkansas.

Tonight, Uncle Tomo was telling his family about the days at Rohwer. He held their attention as his memories sped back through the pages of time.

"We arrived at Rohwer on a hot and humid day in August, 1942. We were very scared and anxious. We had no idea what fate had in store for us. For two days and two nights we rode a crowded and musty smelling railroad passenger car from California to a place that seemed to us like the other side of the world," Uncle Tomo sighed as his story began to unfold.

"We had to leave our homes and jobs behind. Some of us were separated from our family members. My wife's mother lived near us. She was sent to another relocation camp somewhere in the Utah desert. This hurt my wife deeply. I was separated from my favorite sister—whom I never saw again. I never knew where she went, but I know she died there," Uncle Tomo said.

"I was forced to sell my restaurant for only $1,100. It was worth at least $10,000 but I had to take what I could get." He continued, "the government had only given us two weeks to take care of our affairs. This was very little time to sell a business and a house. My wife and I sold everything we had for $2,000. It was a great loss, but some of my friends didn't have time to sell their belongings at all. We were the lucky ones," Uncle Tomo said shaking his head.

Uncle Tomo paused for breath, and then began to speak sadly: "We had no idea what was going to happen to us. We were American citizens, born in the United States. We were Americans who had been betrayed by our own government. Many were very bitter, especially the parents who had sons in the war actually fighting for the United States."

Uncle Tomo paused to catch his breath once again. He took a drink from his coffee cup.

His family was very quiet as he continued: "The train stopped in the Arkansas Delta, two thousand miles from my California home. From the railroad we had a short walk to a sprawling 500-acre compound of Army barracks, barbed wire, and guard towers. We were astonished."

Uncle Tomo continued, "Most of us were American citizens just as much as anybody, and wanted our country to win World War II. Yet, we suspected at least some of the "Kibei" did not share our views."

"What is a Kibei, Uncle Tomo?" asked Norico who seemed to be listening for a change. Uncle Tomo answered, "The Kibei were a group of American-born Japanese who had been educated in Japan. They were believed to be sympathetic to Japan during the war."

Group Photo, Rohwer Relocation Camp, ca. 1943
Photograph courtesy of:
Butler Center for Arkansas Studies
Central Arkansas Library System

"Japan had attacked China, which was a friend of America, and also Pearl Harbor in Hawaii, which was United States territory," Uncle Tomo continued. "Hawaii has since become a state of our Union. The American people were enraged by the surprise attack on Pearl Harbor in Hawaii, and this would cause problems for us."

"Oh! I see," exclaimed Norico, becoming more curious.

"It seemed clear that Japan was intent on conquering the United States. We Americans were fighting Japan, Germany, and Italy all at the same time. That is why we call it a "World War." This war was being fought all over the world, even in England and France. The President of the United States at that time, Franklin Delano Roosevelt, was afraid that the Japanese-Americans would become traitors and help Japan conquer America by spying on the United States," Uncle Tomo explained.

"No place on earth seemed to be safe to anybody. We were afraid to trust anyone, even our own people. This was very sad indeed to those of us who were loyal Americans," he concluded.

"How did the Army treat you Uncle Tomo?" Norico asked. "Did they make you live in a terrible place? What was life like at Rohwer? Did you ever have fun? Did the children go to school?"

"Oh! Oh! One question at a time Norico, one question at a time," laughed Uncle Tomo. He was delighted that his niece was actually interested enough to ask questions.

"At first, we were very scared and worried. We were provided plenty of food, but very few other necessities. It was a terrible time for us. We did not know what to expect next. We had to live in barracks, which contained other families. Several of these barracks were grouped together in blocks," he explained.

He then explained how these barracks were divided into family units or apartments. The buildings were 20 feet wide and 120 feet long. The interior of each building was divided into apartments of different sizes to accommodate both the large and small families. Each barracks housed about twenty-five people, with each of the larger buildings holding about 250 people. A dining hall which could seat about 300 served each group of twelve barracks.

The dining hall was where everybody ate. It was a very large kitchen and dining room. Each group of twelve barracks also had a recreation hall. Also, each barracks had a community building containing bathing, toilet, and laundry facilities.

Uncle Tomo recalled, "We had no indoor plumbing except for this area. The barracks were heated with wood-burning stoves. We also had a large hospital."

Uncle Tomo paused again for a minute. Everyone else remained silent.

Uncle Tomo took another drink of coffee. He sighed, looked down at his hands, then continued, "The Relocation center had a system of self-government, with an elective council, police force, and fire department composed of evacuees, and a detachment of U.S. Army Military Police. These military policemen were there to protect us from local residents who perceived us as a threat. We were not allowed to leave the compound without special permission."

The elderly uncle stood up and walked over to the window. He stared out at the night. His shoulders suddenly seemed bowed. Then he turned around and began to speak again: "For most of us, English was the only language we knew. A few older people could speak Japanese, but we didn't understand them any more than did the soldiers. We sometimes discussed the irony of this. We held much resentment in our hearts to be honest, but we knew we must not voice our discontent. This would only cause more suspicion. The irony of this was that many of our own people were distrustful of each other. We were afraid to voice our true concerns and fears even to our friends. So, we kept our thoughts to ourselves and pretended that everything was okay."

"That must have been a terrible way to live," exclaimed Norico's father.

"Yes, nephew, indeed it was," Uncle Tomo sighed.

"You know, my group published a weekly newspaper, *The Rohwer Outpost*," Uncle Tomo recalled. "Many articles were submitted and read.

Rohwer Relocation Camp Newsletter Masthead, 1943

Courtesy of:
Butler Center for Arkansas Studies
Central Arkansas Library System

Several of the teachers, including myself, donated their time to this community news magazine."

"This newspaper helped us learn the news from the other barracks—such as weddings, deaths, birth announcements, special suppers and that kind of thing. I loved working on this project. I always knew all the current events. Doing something satisfying helped reduce the stress for me," he said.

Uncle Tomo smiled sadly, but Norico noticed his hands were shaking. His memories were bringing back the pain and betrayal of his past.

He continued, "the children went to school just like back home in California. The teachers, most of whom were college educated internees, were very good, at least I thought so, and most of our students excelled. All the adults worked at something regardless of their age."

"What did you work at Uncle Tomo?" Norico's mother asked.

"Well, I did several things," he remembered, "but I mostly taught mathematics. I enjoyed teaching the young people. Some of my friends did other things. Some worked in the hospital or on the numerous farms on the huge tract. They raised vegetables mostly."

"We also played baseball. We had contests of every kind. My favorite competitions were the spelling bees that my students participated in. They usually won because I drilled them so much," Uncle Tomo laughed at the memory, then continued: "The older women worked in a community workroom. They worked on the large looms, making cloth for clothing."

He continued, "I remember being amazed by the beautiful fabrics the older women produced. They made rugs for the floors of their apartments and beautiful tapestries that they used to decorate the walls. We had to do this, because when we left California, the only things we could bring with us were what would fit into a few suitcases. Everything else we owned was sold."

"Yes," murmured Ester, Norico's mother. "My mother taught me to make rugs and tapestries. I still have some."

Norico now listened intently. She didn't know her mother made those beautiful things. She realized that she was learning a great deal.

Uncle Tomo continued, "Do you know the old saying 'Necessity is the mother of invention?' Well, we learned this lesson quickly after arriving at Rohwer. Except for the basics of food and shelter, we had to make everything else ourselves. You would be surprised at the wonders we performed. When we arrived we were only given a cot, a mattress, and three blankets each. Everything else we had we learned to make."

"If we wanted furniture,' Uncle Tomo continued, "we had to make it out of scrap lumber allocated to us by the Army. We would smooth and polish the wood to a beautiful glow. Then we would create chairs, tables or any type furniture we needed. I personally enjoyed working with my hands and made my wife many unusual items. Her favorite was a rocking chair."

"Soon, our little apartment became more like a home, instead of the prison cell that it was. Still, I could hear my wife crying late at night when she thought I was asleep. I knew she was longing for her family and mine as well. Yet, I never let her know that I heard her cry," he remembered.

"Uncle Tomo, tell me about your wife," Norico injected.

"My wife died while we were at Rohwer, Norico. We had been married ten years. I never remarried. Her name was Norico, too. Yes, you were named for her. I am so glad you will be with me tomorrow when we return to the site of the camp. My wife is the main reason I am making this final pilgrimage to Rohwer. I want to lay flowers on her grave one more time. I hear that the cemetery is the only landmark left. I want to see the old place where we shared both bitter and happy memories. I want to plant a cherry tree near her grave and share memories with those who were there with me," the elderly man said quietly.

"I'm very sorry," Uncle Tomo," Norico sighed. "I thought this trip would be awful but I have learned a great deal about my heritage. I think I will understand the Rohwer site when I see it. Thank you very much Uncle Tomo."

Norico's mother and father just nodded, too overcome with emotion for words. Norico, Uncle Tomo, and her parents went to bed, after bidding each other goodnight.

Suggested Reading:

Russell Bearden, "The False Rumor of Tuesday: Arkansas's Internment of Japanese-Americans," *Arkansas Historical Quarterly*, XLI (Winter 1982), pp. 327-339.

Diana Sherwood, "A Transplanted People in Arkansas," *Arkansas Gazette*, March 7, 1943, p. 4

Stephen Steed, "Return to Rohwer." *Weekly Spectrum*, July 8-14, 1992, p.11.

To the North: A Black Family Leaves Arkansas for Work in Michigan

Papa walked slowly into the house as Mama set the table for supper. His face was drawn and tired and he walked as though the weight of the world was on his shoulders. Mama saw him and the smile left her face.

"Jacob, would a cup of coffee before supper help you relax?" she said.

"Yes, Caroline, it would." Jacob replied.

Caroline Jackson poured the coffee for her husband and sat quietly as she saw the worry and stress relax just a bit.

Jacob turned to Caroline and said, "Old man Story really made me mad today. I went to him to settle our yearly wages and I think he cheated me out of three months work. I just can't figure well enough to keep him from cheating us. Oh! I wish I could read and cipher like that old white man."

Caroline stood silent for a minute.

"Jacob, I've been writing my brother Joshua up in Detroit. He thinks if we moved up there you could get a job at a war plant. Do you want me to have him check on a job and housing for us?"

Suddenly excited by the possibility of actually leaving, Jacob admitted, "Yeah! I guess I do, Caroline. At least up there the children could get a decent education at those big public schools."

The next two weeks Jacob went to work in Mr. Story's fields as usual. The last Friday morning that Jacob worked for Mr. Story didn't begin well. Mr. Story seemed to wake up angry. When he saw Jacob in the field he began to yell.

"Jacob, you lazy, good for nothing. Can't you make that hoe move any faster? No wonder you can't make any money, then try to blame me for it."

Caleb, Jacob's young son, was chopping cotton beside his father. He was amazed when he saw his father throw the hoe far into the woods bordering the cotton field. Jacob walked up to Mr. Story, his fists clenched.

"Listen to me, old man!" yelled Jacob. "You have cheated me and my family for years. I can't prove it and I don't pretend I can, but this is the last day you will ever cheat me. I quit and I am taking my family with me."

Mr. Story was stunned. He never expected Jacob to quit! Jacob knew he had made an enemy for life. It was very unusual in 1944 for a black man to "talk back" to his white boss. He expected Story and his friends to make trouble for him—and soon.

Jacob, after rounding up his children, went home. Caroline met them at the door with important news.

"Guess what family! I heard from Uncle Joshua today," Caroline said. "He said if we could come to Detroit now Papa could work at the Flint war plant. He says they are begging for workers and black employees are paid the same as whites."

Black Family, Wilson, Arkansas, ca. 1940

Photograph courtesy of:
Butler Center for Arkansas Studies
Central Arkansas Library System

"Well, Mama, that is certainly good news," sighed her husband. "I just blew up at old man Story and quit. I guess we had better get to packing."

The family worked into the night sorting through their belongings to decide what to take with them and what to leave behind. Long past bedtime, Caleb heard his parents talking and planning on how to make their money stretch until Papa could go to work.

The very next day, the family packed and moved to Detroit. Eli was crying. He didn't want to leave the farm. He begged Papa to leave him with cousin Ben. Papa firmly refused. Early the next morning the family began their journey, all their belongings piled high in the bed of their old pick up truck. They were on the road for three days as they drove from St. Francis County, Arkansas to Detroit, Michigan.

A few days later Caleb sat staring out of the soot-stained window in the bedroom of an old apartment building in Detroit, Michigan. He sat on one of the bunk beds that lined two of the walls. Papa had made the beds for Caleb and his three brothers from discarded lumber he had found in an ally near their apartment.

Caleb knew the room was awfully crowded and often stuffy, but it was better than their tiny unpainted cabin back on the farm. The United States was still fighting World War II. Most housing projects were very close to the war factories. This caused soot and smoke to stain everything including windows and even the freshly fallen snow.

Papa could only find a two-bedroom apartment in the housing project. His job as a maintenance worker in the Flint war factory paid more than he had ever made, but they still had to budget carefully to save toward everyone's education. Papa and Mama shared the other bedroom.

The apartment also boasted a combination living room and kitchen. Mama was always complaining that the kitchen was so small she could hardly do her work for the family of six. Sometimes she would get in a rush and bump her knees because everything was so crowded. Fortunately, the apartment was on the ground floor of the two-story apartment building.

Mama seldom visited with the other ladies in the project. She said she just didn't have time, but Caleb knew it was because she was uncomfortable around city folks. Actually, many of the neighbors were new to Detroit too, having moved from other poor Southern states.

Mama could only find work two days a week at the public school cafeteria. She said that was enough work for a mother of four children anyway.

Papa thought they all had it better than he did when he grew up. All he did was work at hoeing or picking cotton from dawn to dusk. He couldn't even get a decent education. At least their new home was close to the public schools. This meant that his children could get the education that had been denied him.

Caleb knew how his father felt. As crowded as it was, the tiny apartment was a roof over their heads. It was warm in the winter and bearable in the summer. They even had indoor bathrooms. They never had those back in Arkansas. Their cook stove was gas and the icebox kept the food from spoiling.

Caleb was the "scholar" in the family. He read all the time. He was twelve years old and in the seventh grade. He always made straight A's. His goal in life was to become a teacher. Eli was ten years old. He was almost the opposite of Caleb. Eli had always wanted his hands in the soil. He didn't like school. He wanted to fish on his days off. He loved to watch plants and animals grow. He hated the city and often longed to return to rural Arkansas.

The children of the neighborhood laughed at him because he couldn't read well in class. They also made fun of his "country" words. For example he might pronounce "brush" as "brash" or "hope" for "help." He tried to make friends by talking about the animals and crops he had back in Arkansas. This only caused the neighborhood children to laugh at him more. They began to call him "farmer" or "hillbilly" and often mocked his speech.

Papa was after Eli every minute to try harder in school. He desperately wanted his children to be happy. Papa was afraid Eli would run away. True, Eli often looked longingly at the trains passing by on the way back to the South. Caleb also worried about his brother. He tried to keep his younger brother close to him and interest him in school.

Caleb's other brothers, Jeb and Clay, liked school. This made Papa happy, but everybody worried about Eli. Caleb was startled out of his reverie as the sound of a pebble struck the window. He peered out into the street. He saw a group of boys scuffling in the dirty snow.

Caleb came to his feet at once. The boys were ganging up on Eli again. They were holding him to the ground as he kicked and shoved to get away from them. They were making fun of him, calling him names such as "dummy" and "farmer." Eli was kicking and screaming as the boys rubbed the sooty snow in his face. One boy threw a snowball at Eli. It had a rock hidden inside. The rock hit Eli's nose. Blood flew into the dirty snow.

"Do the shoes hurt your feet, hillbilly?" One boy sneered. "Where did you get your funny hat?" another jeered, laughing at the straw hat Eli had worn as long as he could remember.

Eli was crying. Tears and blood ran down his face. He couldn't get away from the boys. They pounced on him, crushing him under their weight.

Caleb ran through the front door and jumped onto the pile of boys. One by one, he pulled them off his brother. They ran away laughing and throwing snowballs at both boys. Eli was still crying, huge tears running down his face.

"I wasn't doing anything to them Caleb. I was just walking along. They ran after me and threw me down. They called me a fool because I can't read as well as they do."

"Are you hurt, Eli?" Caleb gasped, almost breathless himself.

"Only my nose, but I don't think it is broken." Eli whimpered.

"Don't worry Eli," Caleb said. "Mama will take care of your nose. Pay no attention to those bullies. Those kids just don't understand anybody who is different from them. We don't all have the same talents. If we do the best we can to use the talent that God gave us, then we have done enough. Your talent lies in making things grow. That is not a shame or embarrassment."

"You really think so Caleb?" Eli whispered. "Do you think I really should be proud of who I am?"

"Yes, I sure do Eli," Caleb assured him as he put his arm around him for support.

"I thought you were ashamed of me," Eli muttered.

" Oh, no! Eli, I have never been ashamed of you. I know one day you will own a huge farm and make more money than I will teaching school."

The brothers went into the house. Mama had supper ready. She turned from the stove and gasped when she saw Eli's nose.

"How did this happen Eli?" asked Mama as she began to dress his nose.

Before Eli could answer, Papa came through the door from work.

"What happened to your nose, Eli? Papa asked.

Caleb recounted the scuffle while Eli sat silently.

Papa became very angry. "Why can't you fit in, Eli?" Papa shouted. "Why can't you try harder?"

"I don't know Papa." Eli whimpered.

"Papa, this wasn't Eli's fault!" Caleb said, his voice trembling. "I was there!"

Papa looked at the boys. The anger left his face. He sat down slowly.

"I wanted everything to work out here so badly. I wanted you boys to get the education I never had. Papa sighed. Maybe I was expecting too much."

The boys said nothing, just quietly left the room.

Caleb took Eli into their room. He turned on the old battery radio. They listened to "The Lone Ranger." Eli went into the living room when the program ended. Caleb was uneasy. He couldn't exactly say why. The street fight and Papa's comments were on his mind. Caleb sat staring out of the window thinking about his brother. Maybe he was worrying unnecessarily. He heard the train whistle blow. He saw a south-bound train speeding by his window. Caleb realized that he, too, was afraid Eli might run away.

Caleb turned from the window. He noticed a letter from their cousin Ben lying on Eli's bed. He opened the letter and began to read:

> June 6, 1944
>
> Dear Eli,
>
> ".... I know how you feel, people don't like me very well either. They think because I like to write music that I am peculiar. But wait and see, one day I will be famous. You will be too. One day you will come home and buy Mr. Story's farm...."

Caleb thought back to the days when they lived in Arkansas. He could not imagine Eli wanting to return to that. But, maybe Ben's letter would help Eli want a better education so he could one day own his own farm. Caleb remembered how they planted the cotton, weeded (called "chopping") the crop, and harvested the large white cotton bolls in the fall. The work was hard. The sun beat upon their backs and the labor blistered their hands.

Eli had loved working the Arkansas land, but he hated it when it was time to share the crop with the landowner. Eli would love working his own land.

Caleb also remembered other things about Arkansas. Every time he went into Forrest City he saw signs reading "Coloreds only" or "Whites only." These signs were on bathrooms, water fountains, and restaurants. The "separate but equal" saying just didn't ring true to him. At least in Detroit he didn't have to see signs that signified that he was a second class citizen.

Meantime, as the months passed, Mama and Papa grew more satisfied with their new home. Mama usually saved a few dollars each week after grocery shopping and paying the rent. She was happy to be out of the scorching heat and endless rows of cotton and corn. So what if the neighbors were not as friendly as they were back home? They would eventually make friends. They were already getting acquainted with Mr. and Mrs. Williams from across the street.

The Jackson family stayed mostly to themselves. One evening Caleb came home to find Eli sitting in the living room reading a book to Papa! This surprised Caleb and excited him also. Eli was reading about farming, of course.

Papa was very smart to get Eli to read about something he really liked. Actually, to Caleb's surprise, Eli read pretty well.

Caleb listened and encouraged his brother. He showed his brother how to pronounce his words correctly. He was very relieved that Eli had found a way to make himself and Papa happy as well.

"Eli," said Caleb. "Why don't you practice reading to Papa every night? If you will, I will help you plant and work a little garden in the back yard when spring arrives. It will be warm enough to plant next month."

"Yeah!" Papa agreed, "That sure would help your Mama with the groceries. She could preserve vegetables and stretch our budget. This would be wonderful."

"Oh! Yes," chimed in Mama "I would love that. I wouldn't have to go to that expensive supermarket so often."

Eli began to read. The more he read, the more he loved to read. By the arrival of spring, he was an avid reader. He was pronouncing his words just like Caleb. He read books about farming and agriculture—although now and then he would read the cartoon pages from the local Sunday newspaper.

Eli sometimes talked about how as an adult he wanted to grow cheaper and better crops so more people could eat better. Caleb was very proud of his brother.

One evening in late July, the family was sitting on the porch snapping and shelling beans. They heard a loud crash from the back of the house. They also heard loud laughter. Papa jumped up and ran to the back yard.

A gang of vandals had wrecked the garden. Half of the fence had been pushed over. Some of their tomatoes had been uprooted. Beans had been pulled form the ground. Carrots lay uprooted and the corn had been knocked over. The damage was great. Papa was so angry. Caleb had never seen his father, or anyone, that angry.

He ran to the fence shaking his fist and screaming, "I'll get you for this! I'll get you for this! I'll find out who you are if is the last thing I ever do!"

Just then Papa tripped and fell to the ground. His head hit a sharp rock and he was nearly knocked unconscious. He lay on the ground, blood seeping from the wound on his head. Mama ran into the house, crying, trying to find something to bandage Papa's head.

Slowly and painfully, Papa rose to his feet. He didn't utter a word as he began to reset the uprooted plants.

If the vandals hadn't given themselves away with their laughter, the whole garden would have been destroyed. They worked into the night. Their backs were sore and they were very hungry when they finished. Eli sat down on the porch, too discouraged even to cry.

Papa was still very angry. He said they were being persecuted because they were not like everybody else. This wasn't discrimination because of color. It was discrimination because they didn't act and think like their new city neighbors. Their goals were not to work in Flint's war factories all their lives.

The children were willing to save and work for an education. They wanted to use their money to buy books and pay college tuition. Caleb wanted to become a history teacher; Eli wanted to become a farmer, Jeb wanted to become a veterinarian, and Clay imagined himself as a doctor. Each one had a high goal to achieve. But most people didn't understand this and they wanted to destroy their dreams because they didn't have dreams of their own. Papa said that he refused to be punished just because they were trying to make their lives better. He finally went to bed but not to sleep.

Caleb and Eli did not get to bed until after midnight. They could feel nothing but anger in their hearts for the vandals. Eli talked to Caleb far into the night. Discouraged, Eli could not understand why people were so cruel. Caleb didn't know what to say. He just tried to comfort his brother.

Caleb knew that his family would face other problems. But he also knew they would never give up their dreams. He sighed as he snuggled wearingly into his pillow, hoping that tomorrow would be a better day.

Suggested Reading:

Donald H. Grubbs, *Cry from the Cotton: The Southern Tenant Farmers' Union and the New Deal.* Chapel Hill: University of North Carolina Press, 1971

Alexander Yard, "'They don't regard my Rights at all:' Arkansas Farm Workers, Economic Modernization, and the Southern Tenant Farmers Union," *Arkansas Historical Quarterly*, XLVII (Autumn 1988), pp. 201-229.

The End

Printed in the USA
CPSIA information can be obtained
at www.ICGtesting.com
LVHW021412301123
764736LV00012B/158